# *T*wisted *M*agic

## *Raven's Cove Series*
## *Book One*

**By USA Today Bestselling Author**

**&**

**#1 Bestselling British Horror Writer**

**Claire C. Riley**

# lovelasts forever

Georgi
Have a fabulous day
Big love.
C Riley

Twisted Magic Raven's Cove Series
Copyright © 2015
Claire C. Riley

Edited Amy Jackson Editing

Cover design by
Eli Constant Cosmo Constant books
Copyright © 2015

# ABOUT THE AUTHOR

Claire C. Riley is a USA Today and international bestselling author. She is also a #1 bestselling British horror writer. Her work is best described as the modernization of classic, old-school horror. She fuses multi-genre elements to develop storylines that pay homage to cult classics while still feeling fresh and cutting edge. She writes characters that are realistic, and kills them without mercy. Claire lives in the United Kingdom with her husband, three daughters, and one scruffy dog.
Author of:

Odium The Dead Saga Series (post-apocalyptic)
Odium Origins Series (apocalyptic)
Limerence (The Obsession Series) (dark paranormal romance)
Thicker than Blood series (post-apocalyptic romance)
Shut Up & Kiss me (romantic suspense)
Plus much more.

Contact Links:

www.clairecriley.com
www.facebook.com/ClaireCRileyAuthor
http://amzn.to/1GDpF3I

*Dedication.*

*Thank you to hopeless love stories
everywhere.
May they all have happy endings.*

-

Thanks to my wonderful editor, and friend,
Amy Jackson. Thank you for always coming
through for me.

Special thanks goes to all of my Bad-Ass
Girls – Amalie Silver, A. Meredith Walters,
Brittainy C. Cherry, Kelsie Leverich, Stacey
Lynn and TK Rapp, but especially to A.
Meredith Walters, who without her help, this
book would not be what it is. Love you ladies.

And lastly to my wonderful friend, Eli
Constant. She's an amazing mummy, an
incredible author, and a fabulous cover designer.
Thank you for this kick-ass cover, and for your
wonderful friendship, Sow. Love you. #Sorry
#notsorry ooo

# *Twisted Magic*

*Raven's Cove Series*
*Book One*

### *It's a darkness that doesn't want to let go...*

After being banished from her coven five years ago, Sarah vowed to stay away from black magic forever and instead tried to embrace the life of a white witch. However, now a family death has brought her back to her hometown of Raven's Cove, and the good little witch is in line to inherit a powerful gift.

Peter is invisible. Voiceless. Imprisoned in the little cottage in the woods with no way out, waiting for the day that someone will set him free, even as his hope fades. He comes from a coven of white witches, yet was always tempted by the power of dark magic.

Sarah and Peter find themselves drawn together, and they soon learn that to escape the dark magic that controls them, they must first learn to embrace it.

### *Because the only way to rise out of the ashes is to first burn everything down to the ground.*

# $T$wisted $M$agic

## *Raven's Cove Series*
## *Book One*

*By USA Today Bestselling Author*

*&*

*#1 Bestselling British Horror Writer*

*Claire C. Riley*

# *Chapter One.*

The heavy droplets of rain splashed against the darkened windows of my jeep, relentlessly pounding the glass. The bullets of water drenched the ground, creating large divots in the muddy earth.

I blinked, watching the storm through the glass with a mixture of deep anxiety and nostalgia burning in my gut. The little dark stone thatched house nestled within the forest of Raven's Cove was small but intimidating, just like my grandmother had been. But, also just like my grandmother, its size meant absolutely nothing. They were both an oppressive force that could suck the very life from you if they wanted.

It had waited patiently for me to return to it; and now here I was, and there it was. It stared at me and I stared at it.

I let out a slow, burdened breath.

Five years, it had been.

Five long years.

And yet it didn't seem long enough.

I swallowed. My breath was beginning to leave a fog on the windows, making me feel even more trapped than before. But I didn't swipe it away; smudging that blanket of protection, however suffocating it felt, would be pointless. I didn't need to see the house, the windows, the doors, or the little path leading up to it to know what it looked like, to know what waited for me. This place and all that it contained was etched into my memory forever, like a lover's first kiss.

The engine of my jeep still ran, the soft rumble of it still evident even with the heavy rainfall pounding on the roof and the frantic beat of my heart. I squeezed my eyes closed, knowing that I could leave now if I wanted to—just back the jeep out of the driveway and go. I didn't have to stay; I owed them nothing. I owed her nothing.

My coven had taken everything from me, and now, after all this time, they wanted more. Grandmother had died. That wasn't a surprise; she was old—as old as the night, some had said—but what was surprising was that she had left me her home in her will. A home filled with equally fond memories as there were bad ones. The tales that Grandmother used to spin while sitting beside my bed at night tucking me in to sleep were all still there, buried in the thick of my brain and heart. They had never left me, and even now, if I were being truthful, I still thought of them—often in the dead of night when I found it hard to sleep, because it was hard to forget that they were not just tales, but truth. Truth as dark and as cold as slate.

My grandmother wasn't the kind of woman she had led me to believe when I was a young child. Before the dark magic seeped into my life, she was the epitome of love and devotion; and yet afterwards, after I realized the truth of my existence, she was so much more. She ruled my life before I knew any better, and she ruled my life after I did.

Until I was banished.

And now here I was, back where it all started, back at the beginning of my very own story.

"Raven's Cove." I murmured the words, letting their weight travel through me, a heady feeling of strength and desire coursing slowly through my veins upon just saying this town's name. A sense of coming home washed over me, arms wrapping around my shoulders in an embrace, because this was where I truly belonged, whether I liked it or not.

Raven's Cove was ruled by my family, my coven. It was where I was born and raised, it was where I was banished from—where I ran from—a place from which I have hidden. But it was always where I belonged.

My long fingers were curled in on themselves, turning my hands into small, compact fists; my knuckles were white from clenching them so hard, yet I couldn't release them. I thought of her kind and yet wicked face. I thought of all the spells she had taught me, the things that she had shown me right before she had sent me away, and I scrunched harder, letting my nails dig into the palms of my hands until I could feel the bite of pain, and only then did I let go. I was a black witch, yet my heart begged to be different. It didn't like the pain of others; it wanted good and wholesome. It had always wanted light where there was only dark. I was a freak of my coven, of my family.

I unfurled my hands and let out a long sigh before turning the key still dangling from the ignition and letting the jeep lapse into silence. As witches our spirits resided on, even after death—our souls and our magic going back into the earth to fuel not just the current witches but also the next generation of witches. And that was where my grandmother was now, or would be soon: released back into the earth, in every sense of the word, and waiting to give herself to us. After her funeral, her magic would funnel

4

into each coven member, making them stronger and more powerful witches.

I had let her down by turning my back on what I was, I understood that, and our kind held grudges like no other, but she had loved me like I was her own daughter. Despite her banishment of me, I had always known she loved me, but forgiveness for me turning my back on our heritage? Our very way of life? I wasn't so sure.

I swallowed, my heart feeling full and heavy, my head feeling confused. The rain continued to beat down on my jeep, the drumming sound so much louder now that the rumble of the engine wasn't there to mask it. My eyes scanned over the small house, across the garden overflowing with flowers and wild herbs now wilting due to the amount of rain hammering down on them. There was nothing there, I told myself repeatedly, there was nothing there.

They were not there. But of course, if they were not there now, they would be soon enough.

Yes, they would be coming.

And yes, I was afraid.

# *Chapter Two.*

I stepped out of the jeep and slammed the door shut behind me before hurrying up the little stone path and weaving between the flowers and herbs of the garden to the front door. I was soaked by the time I made it under the small canopy above the solid wood door. The rain clung to my clothes and long hair as I fumbled with the old key hanging from the small silver chain around my neck.

I unlocked the door and stepped inside the threshold, but made no further attempt to go deeper. Instead I waited, letting the scents and feelings of years gone by wash over me in a burdensome wave of nostalgia.

It smelled like her.

Like honeysuckle and cinnamon, and I closed my eyes, imagining the sound of her footsteps crossing the wooden floorboards. Her wrinkled hand reaching for me, cupping my cheek in her gentle yet firm grasp as she smiled upon my rain-soaked face. In all the years that had passed, I had never blamed her for banishing me, and I had never stopped loving her. She did what she did to protect me, and our coven. I understood her need to protect, yet I had never understood why she had sent me away. I had mourned the loss of my coven, of my friends and family, and of her.

The image vanished and I opened my eyes, the sting of unshed tears still clinging to my thick lashes. I flicked the light switch, illuminating the room, and I closed the door behind me. I dragged my hand through my hair, pulling the long, damp strands back from my pale face. My eyes grazed over the room, taking in the same old furniture and ornaments that had been there five years ago. My gaze settled on the hearth and the small pile of firewood just next to it and I strode over, leaving a trail of wet footsteps behind me.

I crouched down and built a simple fire, finally warming my hands above the orange and yellow flames as it came alight. I rubbed my hands together, willing the warmth back into them. But it was more than my hands that were cold. It was neither my wet hair nor damp clothing that chilled me. It was memories. Memories and fear.

Slowly, as the heat made its way back into my fingertips, yet not into my soul, I leaned back against the squat brown paisley sofa facing the hearth, dragging the throw blanket from it and wrapping it around my shoulders. I was too exhausted after the long drive to do anything more than sit there and let the fire warm me.

A cold shiver coursed through me as I stared into the orange flames, my hands clutching tightly to the blanket. I hated this place. I hated the memories. I hated the emotions that clung to the very walls of this house like old wallpaper and paint. I hated the misguided actions and ill wills that they still contained. I hated that they knew me better than I knew myself.

But mostly, I hated that I still missed her. I missed everyone, despite everything.

**M**orning sun crept in through the windows, rousing me from my wretched sleep. I stretched, my back feeling stiff from sleeping restlessly on the floor all night. I had awakened every once in a while to throw more wood on the fire and then continued watching the flickering flames in the hearth before drifting back off to sleep.

I sat up, pushing my knotty hair back from my face. My jeans and sweater were still damp in places, making me feel uncomfortable, but my comfort wasn't my main concern just then. I stood up, threw another armful of logs on the fire to keep it going, and I went in search of the kitchen. I needed caffeine to jolt me awake and get me through this day—caffeine and a warm shower. I yawned again, slowly peeling the sweater off me and draping it across one of the wooden dining room chairs as I passed it.

A smile rose to my lips as I entered the low-ceilinged kitchen. It was just as I remembered it: painted a sunny yellow with herbs dangling by the windows to dry out. Pots and pans were stacked neatly by the large black stove, and what seemed like hundreds of chintzy teacups, saucers, and teapots lined the bulky oak dresser by the back wall—and of course, in the middle of the room was the cauldron.

When I was especially little, Grandmother had said she used it to make stews and soups for our large family, but as I grew—and my curiosity along with me—I had discovered that it was so much more than something you cooked in. And when my magic set in at age twelve, I got to use the special black pot to create magic of my own. Of course, back then it was all innocent spells, like turning frogs into bunnies. It was way before the darkness of my coven was truly shown to me.

I walked over to the pot and looked inside it. It was empty, a deep void of hollow blackness apart from the long-ago scents of spells drifting

9

out from it. I took a deep breath, letting their enticing smell pull at me, begging for me to feel them. I knew this place was a poison, and it would kill me if I let it, but it was so hard to resist the pull at times.

I continued to stare down into the pot of blackness, my parched throat burning and my hands itching as I fought to control my urges. I looked away from the cauldron and closed my eyes. If I tried hard, I could almost hear her there, with me, talking me through my spells. Handing me jars and pots with herbs to crush and burn, to tear and boil, to stir into her concoctions and create something beautiful, magical, and addictive. Because that's what magic was—addictive. I understood how my people, my family, became so lost in it. Magic itself was alluring, but dark magic was something else completely.

In the beginning, I wanted what all witches wanted: power. I was strong and obedient, better than most of the girls in my generation. A strong ancestry, a pure bloodline. I got it, and I wanted more of it. I was stronger than my mother, and this was the beginning of the end of our normal mother-daughter relationship. It was her distaste for me, because of my powerful magic, which made me want to eventually change—to be something else, something better. Because power has a way of changing you, of making you chase the dreams that you were not even aware you wanted. I chased them, of course I did, but a dream is supposed to stay free. It's supposed to be just out of your reach to keep you motivated, and if you should catch it—your dream—what then? For me, the dream eventually turned into a nightmare. My mother hated me and I was getting in deeper with something I didn't truly understand.

With a heavy heart I turned away from the cauldron and filled the kettle with water before putting it on the stove and then finding all the ingredients I needed in the cupboards. I brewed the drink and poured myself a large cup before standing at the window to the kitchen and taking a sip of it. The coffee was hot and delicious, a mixture of bitter and sweet, much like life.

I rolled my neck, hearing a crunch come from somewhere between my shoulder blades. I was still deciding if coming back was the right thing to do or not. I had been banished; technically I wasn't allowed back there. But family was family, after all. And who wouldn't attend their own grandmother's funeral? Regardless of the dangers that it would come with. After my banishment, my mother's dislike for me had turned into hate—hate for me, for Grandmother, for everything. She hated me for having the potential to be stronger than she was: to be able to become coven leader if I had wanted. And yet, simultaneously, she hated me more for abandoning it all for a purer magic, and subsequently getting myself banished. I could never win with her.

I finished my coffee, put the mug in the sink, and headed back into the front room. Last night's storm had been strong, but the day was already starting to warm up and I slipped my shoes back on, grabbed my keys, and headed out to my jeep to collect my things. Grandmother's funeral was in two days, and I was stuck here until then. After the funeral I could go back to my life and forget about all of this. Forget about my wicked coven, my grandmother, and forget about the black magic that simmered dangerously inside of me.

The air was fresh outside, the earthy pine scents of the forest assaulting me as soon as I opened the door, and making me smile. I headed to my jeep, trying to avoid the muddy puddles that had been created overnight, though it was impossible to miss all of them. Grabbing my bags from the back of the jeep, I turned to go back inside but stopped at the sound of a raven squawk from a tree next to me. I looked up at it, meeting its gaze head on. Its beady black eyes stared down at me, seeing so far into my soul that I could feel the tendrils of its magic reaching out and scooping up my insides.

"I don't want any trouble." I tried to sound strong, but the quiver in my voice was apparent.

The raven continued to stare at me. Eventually another bird flapped through the trees and swooped down to perch next to the first one. This one was bigger than the other, and I cursed under my breath as they both stared at me.

"Please, I just want to say my goodbyes and then I'll be gone again." I looked away. "I'll give you the house. You can have it all, I don't want it. I don't want any of it."

The raven squawked again, longer and more drawn out than the last time, and the second raven joined in. The bright sky turned dark as their squawks turned to screams and my skin prickled as the sound waves trailed over my skin like deathly fingers. I shuddered just before the sting of claws dug into the flesh on my shoulder and I jerked my head around to look. Nothing was there—at least nothing physical. The screams were louder now, their sounds assaulting me and making me feel sick.

I turned in circles, feeling nauseous and trapped. Caged in like a bird. Dark clouds had gathered overhead, and the once sunny day turned stormy and oppressive. Thunder and

13

lightning began to strike the sky and earth, and rain drenched me in seconds. I ran toward the little cottage, my legs running and yet seeming to go nowhere. Puddles splashed against my ankles and mud drenched my feet and I was gasping for breath. I looked away from the ravens and threw myself against the front door, falling to my knees just inside the doorway with a loud crack. I turned and kicked the door shut behind me as I drew panicked air into my lungs and the cottage began to shake and tremble. Pottery fell from the shelves, pictures smashed against the floor, and the squawks and screams built and built until my eardrums felt like they would pop at any moment. My hands itched to release some of my magic, but I still refused to use it for bad, and I clenched my hands shut.

The noise of the storm outside, the house shaking, pottery falling, rain crashing down, and the steady screams of the ravens outside reached a crescendo, and then the forest abruptly fell into silence so absolute that I couldn't even hear my own breathing.

## Chapter Three

I wrapped the blanket tighter around my shoulders. My body was still shivering from the rain and my coven's abrupt entrance back into my life. At least I knew where I stood with them now—there was no guessing involved. Mother was in control now, and she was not happy to have me back. I hadn't thought she would be, or that I would be accepted by my coven, and yet the facts still stung.

I gritted my teeth to stop them from chattering and knelt down on the floor before reaching over to throw another log into the fire. A scratching sound behind me had my nerves prickling with worry. I turned swiftly, magic automatically teasing at my fingertips, but only came face to face with Whisky—Grandmother's gray and white cat.

She jumped onto the back of the sofa and made her way slowly toward me. She was a miserable and untrusting animal, but who could blame her after all she had seen over the years.

However, she loved to be petted, and I reached out and scooped her up off the sofa and pulled her onto my lap on the floor. She clawed at me and meowed loudly until I began to stroke over her head and ears. I smoothed down her soft fur and her fighting immediately ceased and her cries turned to purrs. It had probably been weeks since anyone had shown her any affection. My own mother certainly wouldn't have made any effort to come in and check on her.

Whisky rubbed her face against me, purring loudly as I petted her, showering her with my affection—affection that we both probably needed. I had loved this wretched old cat when I was growing up, despite her zero tolerance toward children. Seeing her again, petting her, was the best homecoming I could have had given the circumstances, and I smiled down into her face. But instead of another purr, she hissed and wriggled out of my arms before jumping from my lap and back on to the sofa.

I turned to grab her again, but instead my gaze fell to a man.

I gasped loudly and Whisky scratched my hand, forcing me to pull it back. She then strutted off toward the kitchen with a flick of her long tail.

The man leaned against another dresser that stood along the back wall and was filled with yet more of Grandmother's teacups and pottery.

His arms were crossed over his chest, and his short blond hair was hanging a little too long around his ears. He was looking at me, his face blank of emotions.

I watched him and he watched me, our gazes grazing over one another until they met somewhere in the middle and collided. He stood up straight, his nostrils flaring while his eyes flashed with a deep intensity. His stare was penetrating, seeing right through to my very core, yet his expression remained unreadable.

"Who are you?" I whispered out, fear clutching at my throat.

Mother, was all I could think. Mother had sent him for me. I tried to contain the slight tremble in my hands, and I gritted my teeth in defiance. I didn't know how he had gotten in—I thought I had protected myself and the house against her. Regardless, there he was.

His jaw hung slack and his handsome face looked to be drowning with relief. His knees buckled and seemed to give way beneath him, and he stumbled forward a step until he was almost clutching the back of the sofa to keep himself upright. And the entire time, his eyes never left mine. I swallowed, my nerve endings trembling with tension.

I stood up, my hands curling into small fists. "I said, who are you? And what are you doing

17

here?" I kept my voice steady, showing more calm than I truly felt.

Finally, he took a step toward me. "She can see me," he mumbled, more to himself than me. His voice was soft yet hard and I frowned, not sure what to say to that. Because yes, I could see him, but I didn't understand why he seemed surprised by it.

"Yes, she can." I scowled, letting the blanket fall from around my shoulders. "Did my mother send you?" My heart sped up, ramming against my ribcage painfully. "Because I don't care how many ravens she sends for me, she won't scare me away."

Be strong, I thought. Be strong, Sarah. This was just another way of mother warning me, to frighten me and keep me away from the funeral. She had sent him—one of her witch lackeys—to pass a message along, and that message had been received loud and clear.

The man frowned at me, his scowl etched across his face, and then it smoothed out into something resembling elation. "Christ! You can hear me!" It wasn't a question but a statement, a testimony of truth, and I nodded to confirm it for him, all the while watching him in fascination, annoyance, and fear.

There was something about him, something familiar. But like sand, it slipped through my grasping fingers with each reach.

"Yes!" I yelled, annoyance ruling my voice. "Yes, I can hear you and see you. Now get out!"

The man brought his hand up to touch his face, his long fingers caressing his jaw as he spoke. He seemed shocked by the sound of his own voice—but perhaps even more shocked that I could hear him. I noticed that his hand trembled as he moved his fingers across his face, carefully feeling the hard bone underneath and the rough beginnings of a beard above. It seemed as though he were feeling it for the very first time. His voice was rich and deep, a mixture of accents that I attributed to someone who was well traveled, as all witches should be.

Silence descended over the room and I waited anxiously, unsure on what to do next. Would he attack? Would he take me to her? I had no clue, and as the minutes passed I grew more and more anxious. My chest rose and fell with the heavy beat of my heart right before he barked out a loud laugh that made me startle and jump back. His eyes widened and then he purposely laughed again, his eyes caressing my body's every reaction to the sound of his voice.

He stepped forward, and though I wanted to stand firm I unwillingly stepped backwards, not

19

trusting him enough to let him get too close to me. My powers were still there, they had never left, and my palms itched with the desire to protect myself from him. And I would, if need be. But violence had never come as easy to me as it had to others.

He smiled at me, a full smile that showed straight white teeth. "You can see me." His hands moved over his arms and his smile continued to grow. "I can…I'm here." He looked back to me. "You can hear me!"

"What the hell are you going on about?" I asked, my eyes narrowing.

He continued to grin at me like an idiot. A grin that was becoming increasingly irritating.

"Did you hear me?" I snapped, my anxiety at a new level. "Get out, now!"

"You don't remember me?" he asked, his head tilting to one side.

I ignored his comment, not caring who he was. "I want you to leave. Leave now before I hurt you." I held my hands in front of me, letting him see the magic in my palms. His gaze flitted over my palms, instantly dismissing my magic.

"Leave…I can leave." He swallowed, still watching me as a look of indecision flashed across his face. "I can leave," he repeated.

20

"Yes," I nodded, "and I want you to. So get out!" My voice had risen to a new crescendo. Despite my best efforts at not losing control, I was doing just that. Panic clung to me.

He blinked, his hands still moving across his arms, and then he turned and walked out of the room.

I stared at the space where he had been, confusion threading through my veins. What in the ever-loving hell was going on? I was becoming more and more aware that perhaps he hadn't been sent by my mother. He was too shocked to see me—to speak to me—to have been sent by her. Yet if he hadn't been sent by her, then who was he?

I hesitantly followed him, only to find him standing by the kitchen door. He slowly stepped toward it, pausing a mere three steps away before glancing back over one of his broad shoulders. He smiled when he saw that I was still there, watching him, and his eyes held a longing that I couldn't fathom.

He reached out to turn the small round handle, and I stared on in nervous anticipation, wanting to say something—anything—to him, but not knowing what.

I was anxious for him, for me, and for something that I didn't really understand, but the feeling was there all the same. Anticipation fluttered in my stomach as I took a step forward, unsure of what I was going to do next. Grab him? Yell at him?

I watched and waited to see what would happen next, because this was not what I was expecting to happen when I arrived back. I expected angry glares and spiteful words, muttered curses, and of course the damned ravens! And they had come, the ravens—they were watching this house and me, even now—but other than the storm, they had yet to make their move. I was most definitely wrong that Mother had sent this man. I suddenly knew that like I knew how to breathe. My mother knew nothing of him.

He never replied to me, and I didn't bother to ask him again. I wasn't sure what happened next, his body shielded my view, but whatever it was couldn't have been good, judging from the way his shoulders sank and his posture shrunk. I listened to his slow, heavy breathing, the way he seemed to struggle with each breath.

And then he turned around to look at me.

His eyes looked wounded. They hid a thousand pains that I didn't understand. The spark that had been there only moments ago had vanished, and the excitement I had seen earlier was now gone. He appeared…defeated.

He stared at me for a long moment and then looked like he wanted to say something to me— anything—but then, without another word, he left the room.

I stood there for a moment, unsure of what to do next. He seemed sad, broken, almost pitiful. The look he had just given me, it made my chest ache. I thought about shouting after him, but when I opened my mouth to call him, nothing came out.

I didn't know who this man was, and yet the gentle warmth in his eyes and the way his voice instinctively soothed me told me that he wasn't there to hurt me. Perhaps more troubling was that my own deep-rooted instincts told me that somehow, I knew him.

# *Chapter Four*

I hurried after him, stumbling down the hallway to the front door. The downstairs appeared empty, so I headed upstairs to find him. I climbed them two at a time, my bare feet slapping against the wood. My fingers traced along the banister until I reached the landing, where I let go and stood feeling uncertain.

"Hello?"

The cottage was small, and yet just then it felt like an endless maze as I searched each room in search of the stranger.

"Hello?" I called again, louder this time as I made my way toward the first bedroom. I hadn't come upstairs last night. I hadn't wanted to let any more memories in so soon after arriving. I hadn't wanted to revisit my old life, but I guess now was the time, whether I wanted to or not.

I opened the bedroom door expecting the hinges to creak, a sign that no one had been inside since I had left, but only silence met me. Everything was as it had been; not a thing had changed in all the years since I had left. My bed, still made, was by the small window. The white set of drawers still held all the things that I had left behind: my black raven brooch with the small ruby set in it—a sign of my coven, old photos still tacked to my mirror, and my old spell book. They were all still exactly where I had left them.

My throat clenched tightly and I swallowed against the tide of emotions threatening to rise. I blinked away the tears and turned away from the room, and I shut the door behind me just like I had five years ago. Heading in the opposite direction, I checked Grandmother's room and the bathroom. Both of those rooms were empty.

However, Grandmother's bedroom still held her familiar scent, and I took great lungfuls of it in, wishing for the first time in many years that she were here with me. I sat on the edge of her bed, my fingers tracing the floral pattern of her bedding, my urgency to find the mysterious man all but gone, and I finally released the emotions that had been building in me since I had heard about her death. I wept for her loss, knowing that this was the only time I would let myself do such a thing. I couldn't show weakness—not here, of all places.

My grandmother loved me, and I loved her, dearly, but I had no doubt in my mind that she would have struck me down if she saw me crying for the loss of her. She was always so strong, so confident. And no matter how hard I wanted to hate her for sending me away, I couldn't. I loved her despite what she had done, and I loved her because of what she had done.

She would be happy now; soon she would go back to be with the earth and our ancestors, and her powers would flow into the next generation of witches, making us all stronger. I shouldn't have been crying over that. At least, that's what I knew she would say to me if she were still there. Yet the thought only made me cry harder.

Her death was a great service to the coven, which was something that would be rejoiced, only I wasn't a part of the coven anymore, and I didn't want to rejoice her life, I wanted to mourn her death. I wanted her there so I could ask her why she had sent me away. Was it really just because I had begun embracing the lighter side of magic as well as the dark?

Being from a coven of black witches, the fact that I was drawn toward the white ways was perceived as traitorous and unforgiveable. But I had done what I'd felt was best. The darkness had begun swallowing me up, and with each step further into black magic, I had felt myself becoming more and more lost.

I had turned toward the light to save myself before the darkness destroyed me.

A soft mewing noise sounded from the doorway and I looked over, seeing Whisky staring in at me.

"Come here, you wretched thing." I reached out, and she came over, jumping lightly onto the bed and cuddling into my lap with a soft purr. I scratched behind her ears and smiled down at her face, happy that at least I had this small part of Grandmother here with me.

I cuddled Whisky and I let my tears fall. I thought of my life; my friends and family, before I had been forced to give them, and everything that was my life, up. But mostly I thought about the strange man that had appeared from nowhere. There was something familiar about him, but I couldn't work out what. Like a memory just out of my reach, it moved away the more I tried to grasp onto it, until I was left with only a feeling of uneasiness.

Whisky jumped from my lap and I stared after her as she left the room with another swish of her gray tail. My tears had stopped, I realized. My tears had stopped when I thought of him.

I tied my knotty hair into a low bun at the base of my neck and wiped my damp lashes with the back of my hand as I stood back up. Taking a long, deep breath, I left the room, feeling stronger than when I had entered it. Thoughts of him—this unknown intruder—had made me feel stronger. My forehead crinkled in confusion at the realization.

I made my way down the stairs and checked everywhere once more, but still didn't find the strange man from earlier.

I walked back into the living room and sat down in the comfy armchair by the window and looked out upon the forest. All thoughts of the man I had seen left me and I decided that he must have gone out of the front door and I just hadn't heard him. I wasn't wholly convinced that Mother had sent him, and yet I had nothing to truly prove otherwise. If she had sent him, then his message had been delivered. She was strong, stronger than I remembered. And if she hadn't sent him…

I let my worrying thoughts drift, unfinished, because I didn't know how to end them.

The day was sunny again. The storm clouds that the ravens had brought earlier were gone, yet the sunshine gave me no happiness. Instead I thought only of what I had to do next. What I might have to do to stay out of the darkness that surrounded my coven and would, no doubt about it, be trying to tempt me back into it.

I sat and I thought, and I stared out into the trees as I tried to plan, but I had no idea what to expect from the rest of the coven. To them I was a traitor, and they didn't treat traitors well—especially my mother.

I had been a powerful witch five years ago, and the title of coven leader had skipped my own mother and was set to be passed down to me. My grandmother's tutelage and my strong ancestral line had built me up to be next in line for coven leader. I had magic buried deep inside of me—strong magic that I hadn't managed to open up and use yet.

My mother had been incredibly envious. She had never been as powerful as I was, and that had infuriated her.

Yet the more powerful I became, the greater the risk it was to my heart and soul. The blackness began to infect me, and I knew that I had to find the strength to turn away from everything I had ever known. I had to leave it all behind—family, friends, my entire coven, and most importantly, the powerful dark magic that festered inside of me. I had to turn away from the darkness and go toward the light.

I didn't have a choice. Because the person I had been was beginning to slip away and I was terrified of ending up as vengeful and hateful as my mother. Deep down inside I was good. I knew it. My grandmother knew it. The coven knew it. On this fundamental level, I was different from the rest of them. I wasn't content to let the dark take me over.

As a family of dark witches, we were constantly at odds with a coven of white witches, and because of that, my innate goodness was seen as an act of the most horrible treachery.

When I turned away from my darkness and embraced the light, my own coven—my grandmother—banished me.

At first I was glad—happy to be away from the dark and the light and everything in between.

But then I missed it. The magic.

The call of it in my mind.

The tingle in my fingertips.

The power coursing through my veins.

The uttered spells on my lips and the strength that they gave me.

I missed it all.

After I was banished, my grandmother had continued as coven leader, not entrusting my mother to be in control. My mother's blackness was more than just magic, it embraced her heart and soul. Some people are lost to the magic, and my mother was one of them. If she had the power of the coven behind her, there was no telling what she would do.

But now Grandmother's death would bring new leadership. Only I or my mother would be authorized to take the title of coven leader since the coven was descended from our bloodline.

I had no intention of taking it for myself, but she didn't know that, and I knew without a shadow of doubt that Mother would do anything to keep that title for herself. Even if it meant my demise.

I was her only daughter. To some women that meant everything. To my mother—whose dark heart left no room for love—that didn't matter at all. She'd take me down to further her own agenda. If I was in the way, she'd remove me.

# *Chapter Five*

I t was early afternoon and I was stirring some soup in Grandmother's cauldron. It was therapeutic and took my mind off all of my problems as well as the strange occurrences since I had arrived back.

I had barely eaten in almost two days and felt half starved, but of course Grandmother had nothing that I could just nuke in the microwave. Heck, she didn't even own a microwave. So I had started making the soup from scratch, gathering all of the ingredients from the garden and mixing them into her cauldron. As was her usual, the only herbs in the cupboards were the ones used for spells. Having to gather everything was both irritating and worrying; having to go outside with the ravens watching me, and of course it was time consuming. Yet, once back inside the house, I had stared at the herbs and vegetables with a satisfied smile on my face.

Grandmother had loved gardening. It was quite possibly one of the only traditional grandmother things that she did. It was a wonderful feeling seeing her hard work still paying off, even after her death.

The soup was almost done and it smelled delicious. My mouth was watering as I poured myself a large bowl and sat down at the small table and chairs in the kitchen to eat it. I had showered and dressed in fresh clothes, and despite still feeling tired after a terrible night's sleep on the floor in front of the hearth, I felt better prepared for what lay ahead. After eating, of course.

I lifted the spoon up and blew on it before sipping the soup and burning my mouth despite my carefulness.

"Ouch," I hissed, taking a drink of water to soothe my tongue.

His quiet laugh startled me and I dropped the spoon, sending soup sploshing over the sides of the bowl. I looked up sharply, seeing him in the doorway between the living room and the kitchen.

"You're back," I stated, glaring at him.

He raised an eyebrow, the corner of his mouth quirking upwards. "And you can still hear me."

"Well, I still have ears," I snarked. "Who are you? And why are you here?"

I placed my hands on the table, palms up, letting my magic dance between my fingers like

33

a small ball of glowing ice. I had decided that I wasn't going to take any chances—with him, with my mother, with anything. If I had to fight dirty, I would. So long as I made it through the next two days and got away from there in one piece.

He watched my glowing hands for a second before looking back to my face with an almost bored expression. "I'm Peter, and I'm guessing your grandmother, the wonderful Violet, never mentioned that I came as part of the furnishings." He sneered as he said her name, and my magic sparked and fizzed.

"I don't know what you're talking about, but if you speak about her again in that tone, you'll be sorry." I held his stare, forcing him to look away first.

"You can't hurt me, Sarah," Peter said, stalking further into the kitchen.

"Your first mistake would be to assume that," I replied, not letting him know how intimidated I felt, especially by the fact that he knew my name.

He came closer and his eyes darted from me to the soup and back again.

"Look, I don't know what you're doing here, or what kind of deal you had with my grandmother, or my mother, but I want you to leave—in fact, I insist that you leave, right now." He didn't reply, his eyes were now totally fixed on my soup. "Are you even listening?"

"Not really," he replied bluntly.

My eyes narrowed at his words. "Well you had better st—"

"Tell me how it tastes," he interrupted me, his voice full of longing.

"What?"

Peter looked up at me impatiently. "Tell me how it tastes, the soup. Describe it to me."

My mouth opened and closed in shock, and Peter crossed his arms in front of him. His hair still had that disheveled look about it, his face rugged with a hint of anger. But his eyes were different. Yesterday they had been filled with hope and warmth, with a touch of desperation.

Today they were cold. Empty.

He shook his head and looked toward the window. "You really have no idea what you've gotten yourself into by coming back here, do you?"

I started to answer him, but realized that I had no real response, so I closed my mouth and let my gaze follow his out the window. My stomach growled in protest, wanting the food in front of me, and yet mentally, I had lost my appetite.

"Who are you?" I gritted out. "And what are you doing here?"

"It doesn't matter."

"Who sent you?"

"No one."

"How are you even getting in? I protected this place." I snapped feeling exasperated.

"I was already here."

My gaze burned into his at this revelation. "What do you want?"

"From you? Nothing." He dismissed me quickly with one brief glance.

Silence descended between us again as I waited for him to give me something more, but his mouth remained shut.

"That's it? That's all that you're going to tell me?"

"What else do you want to know about me, Sarah?" he huffed out impatiently.

I stared at him, wide-eyed. "How do you know my name?" I whispered, my eyes searching his face for something, anything. "Please tell me if she sent you. Please." I sounded weak, desperate, and I hated myself for it.

"No one sent me here for you," he replied, his soulless eyes finally looking back at me.

"Then how…"

"Am I getting in here? I already told you, you're just not listening to me." He crossed his arms and looked away again.

I gritted my teeth, trying to calm my frantic heart. I didn't understand what he was telling me, but if what he was saying was true then my protection spell was still in place. Slight relief washed through me at the thought—despite the obvious questions still unanswered on who he was.

I watched him through curious eyes, a familiarity settling inside of me. "Do I know you?" I asked cautiously.

He held my gaze, his eyes widening in shock and then narrowing once again. "You tell me, Sarah," he replied vaguely. "Do you know me?"

I frowned as I looked at him—really looked at him. At his hands that looked so strong, at his warm eyes that both heated and cooled me. I watched him like I knew him, a sense of something burning in my gut, and yet nothing came to my mind. I cleared my throat and looked away from him, dismissing the strange feelings.

"You know my name," I said instead.

"I know a lot about you."

I looked back sharply, watching his mouth turn up into a sneer.

"Violet never stopped yapping about you."

I wondered why I irritated him so much. Every time my name or my grandmothers were on his lips, he turned cold, hard and uncaring. I couldn't help but wonder what had made him this way. This man that knew who I was, and yet was a stranger to me.

"What else did she say about me?" I asked, my tone urgent.

Peter laughed darkly. "What is it you'd really like to know, Sarah?"

I sucked in a breath, feeling like my name on his lips was an echo from another time and another place. It was there, so close, and yet...he looked away and the connection was gone. Lost.

"I want to know about my grandmother. You obviously knew her."

He looked back briefly and purposefully rolled his eyes before dragging his hands over his face in exasperation. "Jesus, I hate this family." Peter took a step back and shoved his hands in his pockets. "No, you want something that I can't give you. You want to know what she said about you—if she loved you right up until her bitter, wretched end. That's what you want to know, isn't it?"

He was almost yelling and tears welled in my eyes, because yes, that was exactly what I wanted to know.

"Isn't it, Sarah?" This time he did yell, his voice louder than the rushing in my ears.

"Yes!" I cried out, the tears tumbling free. "Yes, that's what I want to know," I sobbed.

I was embarrassed by my reaction to him, to his anger and the way he made me feel like a stranger in this house. I wanted him to leave, to get out of this house and away from me. And yet, the words couldn't leave my mouth. They were stuck. The words buried deep beneath my shame for baring such intimate emotions to someone I didn't know.

How could he bring me to tears?

How could he know how to hurt me?

And why did it feel like I had heard him shout before?

His mouth was a thin hard line, his eyes narrowed and never losing focus, unlike myself.

"At the end, she never even mentioned you. That's how much you meant to her. She was a selfish, evil bitch, who even at the end only ever cared for herself and her coven," he replied before turning and walking away from me.

# Chapter Six

Peter.

She had been crying for what seemed like hours. Though it could have been minutes for all I really knew.

I flattened my hands over my ears, trying to drown out the sound of her sobbing, but it did little to help. I had gone too far, I had unwillingly pushed her into this sadness and grief, and this was my punishment: having to listen to her wail for hours on end.

If I were being honest, I would have admitted to the guilt I felt for hurting her. That the crack of her heart had been almost audible from across the room as I fed her lie after lie.

She didn't deserve it. This wasn't her doing. She hadn't locked me in this damned house for all eternity. But I couldn't help the bitter anger that snaked up my spine and curled around my heart any more than she could help her tears.

It was the darkness.

The black magic of this house which poisoned everything that it touched.

And it was me. My anger. My bitterness. My sadness.

Sarah was even more beautiful now than she had been five years ago, and nothing at all like her wretched grandmother, or her sadistic mother. She was the anchor to my sanity, and the only thing keeping the light in me alive when all seemed lost.

Her hair was thick and long, begging for my hands to wrap themselves in it. Her face was striking, as if sculptured from porcelain. But it was her eyes that called to me—it had always been her eyes. They held such ferocity. She had never been afraid of anything, always so strong.

But it didn't matter.

In the end, none of this mattered.

I was forever a bystander to everything and everyone. I couldn't touch or feel, I couldn't taste or smell.

And I couldn't escape.

Even with Violet's death, I couldn't escape.

Violet had made sure of that.

And all because I had fallen in love with Sarah.

*

*"What are you staring at, Peter? Get up here."* Sarah smiled as she continued to climb the tree and I followed up closely behind her.

*I caught up with her easily; my legs were much longer than hers—a fact I was proud of. I would be a tall man, broad and strong like my father. I hooked my leg over a high branch and settled there waiting for her to catch up to me. I couldn't help her—she wouldn't allow it. She was too proud to accept help from anyone—a fact I admired in her.*

*She finally made it up to my branch and she mimicked my actions, straddling the branch like a horse and gripping the branch next to her for support. We stared silently over the meadow, watching the trees swaying and the leaves rustling. It was peaceful and beautiful.*

*I glanced across to her, and I watched her cheeks rise in a smile.*

*"You're staring again."* She grinned and turned to face me, the sunlight glinting off her raven-black hair.

*I reached out, my fingers gliding gently over it, and she blushed.*

*"Can I tell you something?"* I asked, rubbing the back of my neck.

*"Anything,"* she replied simply, easily.

*I wet my lips and took a breath before speaking, knowing that it was now or never. We had been friends for so long that I didn't know what life was supposed to be like without her. We did everything together, despite having to do it all in secret.*

*Our families hated one another. I was from a coven of white witches, supposed to be pure and good, and Sarah was from a coven of black witches.*

*We weren't allowed to be friends.*

*We weren't allowed to be anything more.*

*Because we weren't supposed to be anything other than enemies.*

*But then life didn't always work out like you planned it.*

*"I'm going to ask you to marry me one day, Sarah Leigh," I finally said, the words leaving me in a rush. Like the wind through the branches of a tree, they seemed to flutter and fall between us, and I waited eagerly to see where they landed.*

*She smiled again, that smile she has that was just for me. "I know, Peter." She turned to look back at the meadow. "And I shall say yes."*

\*

43

"Will you shut up!" I yelled down to her, regretting the angry words as soon as I said them. Because I hated myself, not her, and I was angry at her grandmother, not her. But the rage that burned inside of me, god it was killing me. Sucking the very life from my veins.

"I'm sorry." I mumbled, dragging my hands through my hair. "I'm sorry, I didn't mean it." She couldn't hear me, no one could hear me.

I expected her to continue crying, expected nothing in return, for my voice to go unanswered and unheard like it had so many times before.

But instead she went silent and I froze, staring down at the dusty wooden floorboards. Staring as if I could see right through them to her.

For the past ten years only Violet had been able to see and hear me, and yet now everything had changed. I wondered why, after so long. Perhaps because Violet was dead now. I still held onto the hope that the magic would fade and I could leave, though yesterday had been a soul-crushing disappointment. Violet had said that no one would ever hear my voice again, that no one would ever lay eyes on me or feel my touch.

She had sworn that I would be trapped there forever. Alone.

And so far that had been true.

Yet now things had changed. She was finally gone, and Sarah had come back home, and after ten years of feeling nothing, I could feel things again.

I could feel my hair, my face, and my own damned hands. I was once again a man with a body. But it still wasn't quite enough. I still couldn't feel the world around me.

Sarah's magic was powerful enough to give me a taste of what I had been missing. But only a taste.

I was a white witch and I had been raised to be kind and good. To forgive easily. But over the years, loneliness had made me bitter, and I had embraced my darker, angrier side. I was a good witch turned bad. Yet the bad had always been inside of me, much like the good had always been inside Sarah.

It remained quiet downstairs, and I thought about going to check on her. But I couldn't. My shame at losing my temper and shouting at her was too much.

Besides, she didn't know me, or who I was. She had no idea that our lives had been entwined since before either of us were born.

She had no idea that I had fallen in love with her so long ago.

And she had no idea of the pain I felt when she stared at me so blankly, our love so unbelievably lost to her.

So instead of going down, I paced the floor and stared out the cracked and dirty attic window, watching the trees sway with the cool autumn breeze. Watching the sunlight glistening on the muddy puddles. Watching the birds flitting to and fro. And I wished with all my heart that I could be outside, feeling the sunlight on my skin, the wind in my face. I wanted to smell the air after it rained, and to feel the rain soak my hair. I wanted to feel everything.

A sad tear trickled out of my eye and I swiped it away angrily. I was sad and I was angry.

But most of all…I was lonely.

I t was nighttime, and the moon was out and hanging heavy in the darkened sky.

The house was still quiet, so I finally made my way downstairs, hoping that Sarah was sleeping and I wouldn't have to speak to her.

My own emotions had been on a rollercoaster since she had returned. The joy at seeing her safe and well again had given way to shock and amazement that she could finally see and hear me. But the realization that I was still trapped and that her memories of me were still gone, had set free all of the slowly festering anger that had been burning inside me. I still couldn't leave, and she still didn't know who the hell I was.

Ten years ago, we had been so close to discovering a dark family secret together. We had been in love. But then everything had changed. I was imprisoned, and she was spelled by her grandmother to forget me and eventually sent away as a precaution…to make sure she never remembered me or the secrets we had been uncovering.

A piece of me died that day.

I didn't care about the magic, the secrets, or the lies; I only cared for Sarah.

My love for her still burned brightly, yet she felt nothing. She remembered nothing. But at least she was safe. At least my loneliness served a purpose—it kept her safe. And then she was banished, sent away, and Violet said I would never see her again.

I walked silently into the living room and found her curled up on the sofa, her eyes closed. A blanket was draped across her stomach and falling onto the floor. The fire had begun to die down, and I had the urge to throw some wood on it for her, to keep her warm through the night. But I couldn't. Because I couldn't touch the wood, nor could I pull the blanket higher up her body. I couldn't do anything to help keep Sarah warm. I couldn't protect her, the love of my life, from anything—not even the cold.

My eyes traced the smooth curves of her collarbone and shoulders. The way her pale skin contrasted with the navy blouse that she wore and made her look even paler, her skin even smoother. The way her hair fanned out across the arm of the ugly sofa. The way her pink lips were parted fractionally, allowing the air to enter and leave as she breathed quietly.

As I watched her, the anger I held inside of me faded, as it seemed to do when I looked at her. She was the soothing balm to my broken heart.

I stood in front of her, but I cast no shadow. I stood in front of her a lonely man, and I wanted to wake her. I wanted to apologize to her for the hurtful things I said earlier, for the fact that I'd made her so sad. Because I could see that her eyes were still puffy from crying—crying because of things I had said, and it made me ache to think that I'd caused that. I loved her so much. I had always loved her, yet this so-called life that I led, this hell that I continued to endure, was changing me. I was turning into a man I didn't recognize. A man she would hate.

I reached over to tuck a stray lock of hair away from her face. It was an automatic movement, and something I did without even thinking. But of course I couldn't touch her; I could only watch her.

The anger was gone, replaced by devastation.

I staggered sideways, struggling to breathe because I felt so desperate for this to end, to be over.

I sucked in air over and over, but it did nothing because I was nothing.

I wasn't here. I wasn't there. I wasn't anywhere. And I would always be nowhere.

The hope I had felt when Violet died was gone now that I knew her death hadn't broken my curse. That I was still trapped in this stupid fucking house. And the one woman that I had wanted to see for all those years was, in fact, the only person that could see me. But that she didn't remember me, or the things we had shared.

It was a bittersweet torture.

I turned away from Sarah and stared into the fire, still breathing in and out so fitfully that I was gasping, yet the air still never made it all the way down. I felt dizzy and sick and sad. But mainly I just felt so, so angry again.

"Peter? Are you okay?"

Her soft voice was like a beacon in a storm, and I clung to it as the blackness that was suffocating me tried to pull me under. I swallowed, my emotions getting the better of me. How could I love her so much and yet despise her at the same time?

The urge to lash out and say something to her to make her understand was drowning me. Because no, I was not okay. I wanted her to hurt, to make her feel the pain I was feeling, because how could she not remember me? How? How could I be in so much pain at her loss, when she felt nothing for me?

I wanted her to understand who I was, what we had been to each other. The hopelessness was building into a frenzy inside of me, but I knew I wouldn't say anything…couldn't say anything, not if I truly loved her. Because it was better for her not to know about any of this; it was safer for her. She'd be gone in two days' time and I would be on my own again. I would suffer this misery for both of us. For eternity.

She could live her life free of burden, and wasn't that what love really was? If I truly loved her, shouldn't I set her free?

Because no matter what, we could never be together.

"Can I do anything? Can I help?" Her voice was desperate and urgent, and I felt even worse because she sounded so genuinely sad for me, like she really wanted to help. I had made her cry because I was a bastard. Because I was bitter and angry, and yes, because I needed her to not remember me. And yet she was still trying to comfort me, after everything.

But she couldn't…

She couldn't…

She couldn't…

I had to do this alone. I had to keep her safe.

I turned around to face her, my feelings laid bare, naked on my face for her to see. My torment apparent. I wanted my freedom back. I wanted Sarah back. But I couldn't have either.

Because if Sarah remembered me, that meant the truth had come out and we were all doomed.

"You can't help me," I said, sounding as though I were strangling. And maybe I was.

Her pale hand reached for me, to try and offer comfort that she couldn't possibly give.

"I'm sorry, Peter."

I could see it in her face that she didn't understand what she was apologizing for. She was saying sorry, for the sake of saying it.

Her hand was still there, poised between us, trying to close an infinite gap that could never be filled. A void which would forever be endless. Her eyes were glassy, but if she cried again I thought I might just vomit, because I didn't want to see her pity or her guilt or her sadness; I had enough of my own. So I backed away from her. She looked hurt. But I didn't care.

I didn't care…

…But of course I did.

It was this place—it was driving me mad. It was sending me to the brink, and by god I hoped I fell over into it so that the nightmare ended. Because then perhaps I wouldn't have to remember. Maybe I would forget the truth of who we were and what we meant to each other. Maybe then I wouldn't need to do the right thing and I could tell her the truth and be damned with the consequences. My love for her was eternal, I lived and breathed my love for her, but the blackness inside me was choking my soul. Strangling me like a viper wrapped around my heart. I was bitter and full of hate. If it weren't for the strength of my love for her, I would be lost to the blackness within me.

"I hate this family," I said, and she nodded in agreement.

"I understand."

I sneered at her. "You don't know anything."

Pain. That's what I felt when I hurt her. Pain, like a knife in my side. A dagger to my heart. A blade in my chest. Pain. Burning hot pain. But I wanted her to hate me, to despise me. Because it would make this all so much easier if she did. If she wasn't so kind, so caring, and so reminiscent of the woman I loved. Because Sarah didn't hate, she forgave. She always forgave. And she always cared.

And if I hurt her and I could get her to hate me then perhaps she would leave before I gave in to my temptation. Perhaps it wouldn't hurt so much when she looked at me so blankly, so fucking clueless to what we were to one another.

Her eyes were sad again, and I knew that I had done that. Once more I had hurt her, and I had to try and make myself remember that it wasn't her fault. But beneath her sadness, I saw something else—something I didn't want to see.

We were magnets, and we were drawn to one another. There was an attraction there, no matter how angry or sad we felt, and though she didn't remember it, she loved me too. Deep down, buried beneath everything else…

…her memories may be stolen, but her feelings lived on.

But we would destroy each other in our fight to stay together, so I needed to set her free. I dug deeper to hurt her, to really hurt her. To make her feel me. To make her dislike me so much that she wouldn't remember me when she left.

And though I loved her with every ounce of my being, the blackness inside of me thrived on her pain.

"I hate you," I spat out.

She flinched and a sick part of me liked it. I liked the flash of pain that crossed her face, the snuff of hope that died in her eyes. I liked it, because it was the right thing to do. It would keep her safe. It would push her away from me.

"I hope you suffer before they kill you," I said, forcing away the remorse. The guilt. I hated to hurt her, but I had to. Even if it ripped me up inside.

And it worked. I could see the moment my words hit and burrowed deep. She didn't know me, but she was still affected by the seeming hatred that I threw at her.

She couldn't know that I didn't even mean it.

Not at all.

Not even a little.

I just needed her to hate me.

I just needed her to never remember how much she had once loved me.

# *Chapter Seven*

S arah.

P eter stared at me, and though I didn't know him, I could tell that he didn't mean what he said. But it still hurt. Because I feared he was right. I could see the truth in his nasty words. I would most likely suffer before the coven killed me—if they killed me. They'd make sure of it. They'd take delight.

But then my fear turned to anger, and that was much easier to stomach.

"Get out," I whispered through clenched teeth. "Get out, now." No, I didn't believe he meant it, but that didn't make it okay.

He laughed loudly, but there wasn't even the hint of amusement in his laughter. It was full of pain and anger and wretchedness. It was the most horrible laugh I had ever heard. I wanted to cover my ears to block it out. It made me feel off balance. And even stranger, it made me want to comfort him. Because his pain hurt me. I felt it deeply. I wanted to comfort this horrible stranger who had made it his mission to make me miserable. I didn't understand my feelings. And I didn't like them.

He stopped laughing and looked at me. "Believe me, I would if I could, but Violet saw to it that I wouldn't be going anywhere."

My magic tingled in my fingertips and I stared at him.

"What do you mean?" I demanded, wanting answers. He was being purposefully evasive and I was tired of it.

"Your good ol' grandma trapped me here. I can't leave. I can't speak. I'm a shadow. A phantom. I'm absolutely nothing!" he shouted and I forced myself not to cower in the face of his anger.

"You're trapped? I don't under—"

"Does it matter? I can't leave. You're stuck with me, princess, so deal with it," he interrupted, all but snarling. "You're stuck with me until you leave."

He was trapped. Why? Who was he and how had it happened? It was obvious from his hatred toward my grandmother that she was the one responsible. I wanted to pepper him with a million questions. I wanted to badger him into honesty, but I could tell by the look on his face that my playing interrogator wouldn't be appreciated. And I knew instinctually that I needed to tread lightly. Something bone deep directed me and how I should react toward this man standing angrily in my living room.

So I swallowed my questions, saving them for later, but I made a decision to do everything I could before I left to free him from the house. Not because I pitied him—something told me he wouldn't appreciate that useless emotion from me—but because he was a void. A black void that was filled with bitterness and grief.

It tainted the walls that should otherwise have been filled with bittersweet memories. I wanted to set him free because he didn't belong there. It was wrong. An abomination. I felt the wrongness of it buried deep within me.

I didn't want to waste any time, so without another word to Peter, I went upstairs and headed straight to my grandmother's room. I knew that my spell book would be no good; I would need Grandmother's spell book for this.

I could hear Peter's footsteps trail after me, but I didn't wait for him to catch up.

I went into her closet and stood on my tiptoes, reaching to the top of the far back shelf, and I felt around for the thick book she used to keep there. I grunted with the effort, ignoring Peter when I heard he came to stand in the doorway of the closet.

My fingers finally touched upon the old book and I pulled it down. It wasn't dusty like I expected it to be. Instead it seemed like she had used it only yesterday, and that left an uncomfortable pang in my heart.

Frowning, I looked up at Peter, hating that he was still watching me, his eyes cold and his mouth a straight line of contempt. I stepped forward and he stepped back, out of my way, and I wondered if he hadn't moved, could I have walked right through him.

I sat down at Grandmother's desk and tried to open the spell book. The pages seemed to be glued shut with magic. I wasn't surprised—not really. It was basic security necessary for witches to protect against our enemies.

I tried to think of what spell my grandmother would have used to open it when it finally hit me. I chanted my incantation quietly, watching as the magic dispersed from the cover like a fog, and I couldn't help but smile. The spell was a silly rhyme that she had sung to me as a child, and one I still recited to myself when I missed her.

I opened the cover and stared down at the pages, flipping through the entire book and finding the same phenomenon all the way through: empty page after empty page.

I tried the incantation again, but to no avail. I took a deep breath and laid my palms against the book and began muttering a stronger spell. My magic stung the tips of my fingers as it left me, wrapping itself around the book like vines. I spoke louder, urging the words to come forth from the pages, but still nothing. I stopped the spell and stared down at the book in frustration, realizing that this could only be removed by the owner.

I pressed hard against my temples and tried to rub away the beginnings of a headache. I was unsure of what to do now. Peter was right there, next to me, watching my every move, and it was making me nervous.

"Will you go away?" I muttered without bothering to look up.

"I told you, I ca—"

"I know what you said, but you can go away from me. That's not impossible, is it? You don't have to watch my every move." I bit on my bottom lip and closed the book with a sigh.

"What are you doing?" he asked, ignoring my request.

Rude, aggressive, heartless. In my head I listed all the things I disliked about this man. It was my version of counting to ten; acknowledging his faults made them easier to bare.

"Don't ignore me, tell me what you're doing." His tone was panicked and also irritable. As if the fear that perhaps I couldn't hear him anymore was attempting to outweigh the very thought I would ignore him.

I huffed, letting him know—in my own way, that I could hear him, but I didn't care to talk to him right now. Silence fell between us. The only noise was that of our soft breathing. I stared down at the book, feeling tired and hungry, but most of all beaten—like everyone was one step ahead of me. It was a miserable feeling.

"You should go get some sleep," Peter suggested, his voice deep and rich, almost caring.

Turning abruptly in my chair, I glared at him. "You should get some sleep!" I retorted with a glare, causing him to bark out another humorless laugh. I shook my head at his obstinacy. "Just go away."

"I can—"

"I know!" I shouted, throwing my hands in the air. With an angry sigh I turned away from him and stared back down at the book. The pages were old and yellowed, the corners turned up at the ends. The cover was frayed and the writing faded. It was just how I remembered it. I closed my eyes and put my head in my hands.

"I can't sleep," Peter said suddenly, his voice soft.

"So count sheep," I muttered.

"No, I mean, I physically can't sleep. I never sleep. Not now, anyway."

I pressed the heels of my palms against my eyes so hard that I could see colors flashing behind my closed lids. I dropped my hands and slowly turned in my seat so I could see him.

I took the time to really look at him—this stranger that was stuck in my grandmother's house and seemed intent on driving me insane. This man who had just told me that he couldn't sleep. Ever. He was a mystery. A riddle. He was annoying as hell. But at least he was nice to look at.

His jaw was strong and defined, with the dark shadows of a beard that I'd noticed he rubbed absently when he was angry or upset. Like he was doing now. I strangely wished that I was his hand. That I was the one feeling his flesh and bone beneath those fingertips. To caress his rough skin and feel him relax. Because the desire to soothe him, or offer him some kind of solace, overwhelmed me. I didn't know if things would ever be okay—certainly not for him—but I wanted to stop that look of pain in his eyes and give him some hope.

The feeling was disarming to me. But I didn't cave to the instinct; I didn't trust it. How could I? It was completely irrational.

"I haven't slept in ten years. It's the spell. What I wouldn't give to dream again..." he said, his words trailing off, and he looked away, closing his eyes briefly, his words sounding shameful.

I felt a wave of disgust for my grandmother just then. It was so strong and so real that it left me feeling sick inside.

I didn't understand why she had done this to Peter, and I couldn't say with any certainty that perhaps he didn't deserve it, but I could say that it didn't feel right.

I glanced back at Peter and found him sitting on the very edge of her bed, as if hating that he had to sit there at all. His body was tense. His shoulders rigid. His hair had fallen over part of his face, shielding it from my view. But I didn't need to see his face to know how he was feeling. It was plain to see, and I felt his pain as if it were my own. His anguish and frustration burned through my veins, and suddenly I found myself not angry with him anymore. How could I be? He was a victim. That much was obvious.

"I'm sorry," I said sincerely. "I really am. Please don't..." I didn't know how to finish my sentence to him, but when he looked up, his messy hair falling away from his face, I knew he understood me without me having to voice my words.

Please don't be cruel. Don't hurt me. That's what I was begging him with my eyes. I didn't feel strong just then. I felt weak, fragile. Ready to break into a thousand pieces. I couldn't stand his cruelty, especially when I could see he didn't even mean it.

His expression was a mask of guilt and suffering. "I'm sorry," he said quietly and then looked away.

Rubbing my hands together, I wrung them out in front of me as if I could shake out the magic that was itching through them. I felt uncomfortable. Restless. Peter was making me feel twitchy and wired. I rubbed the tips of my fingers together over and over again as I tried to soothe the irritation. And he watched me all the while. His gaze intense and unreadable. I finally stopped, feeling self-conscious.

"I was trying to find the spell that she cast. The one that trapped you here," I said, deciding to stop being such a bitch and let him know what I had been trying to do. Perhaps that would comfort him somewhat.

His eyes connected with mine, and a spark filled them once again. It was the same look I had seen on his face the day before, in the kitchen, when he'd realized that I could see and hear him.

Then I felt the guilt. Because I shouldn't give him such a false sense of hope when I wasn't sure I could help him. The stupid spell book was empty and I didn't know if I could change that.

So I should have kept my plan to myself. But I had wanted to do anything, say anything, to erase the pain on his face. It had been an irresistible compulsion. I hadn't been able to fight it. I just knew that it was necessary for me to help him. To save him.

Because he should never experience that sort of pain. It was an absolute. I didn't know where the thought came from, but there was no altering it.

He gifted me with a smile that took my breath away. Once again I felt blindsided by how I felt about him. The intensity of my emotions took me by surprise.

We were two souls, trapped, each in our own way, and cursed by my wicked family. Perhaps it was only that I saw my own agony echoed in his that made me feel connected to him.

He swallowed, his Adam's apple bobbing up and down. His hands were clasped together tightly in his lap, and I startled at how our reactions mirrored each other's.

"Do you think you can?" he asked after a beat, his voice thick and heavy.

"I don't know, but I'll try," I answered honestly.

His gaze had me cornered, backed up until I had nowhere to go. The edges of his mouth turned up in a brief flash of a smile, and I couldn't help but smile back. I liked the unspoken thanks that came from that attempt at a smile. I realized that I would do anything to see it again.

"You could leave then, be free," I added, my words a whisper.

"I'd like that," he replied, the first real truth he had spoken.

"You'd never have to see this wretched family again," I joked, but he didn't find the humor in it. In fact, he looked pained by the thought.

Silence stretched between us and heat crawled up my cheeks. I cleared my throat, giving myself enough time to think of something to say that wasn't completely stupid. Because this damned silence was making me feel...strange and uncomfortable. Like he was attempting to communicate something to me that I wasn't quite able to catch.

"I don't think you should set me free." He said, his words almost a whisper.

"Don't you want to be, Peter?"

"Like you couldn't imagine." His voice…full of so much pain.

"Then let me help you, please." I pleaded.

He didn't reply, but the confusion, the war waging inside of him because of his indecision was clear to see.

"You should leave, Sarah." He swallowed, his face twisting in disgust as he said, "you need to leave here, forever."

I rolled my eyes at his statement, having no intention of leaving here before my grandmother's funeral. Mother hadn't been able to scare me away, and neither would he. So instead I moved on to something else, something which I needed to ask.

"Can I ask you something?" I said, wanting to look away from his gaze but finding it harder by the second. I felt almost naked in front of him, like he could see all the silly thoughts that were running around in my mind. Thoughts that were private and mine.

His gaze washed over me—from head to shoulders, down my legs and to the tips of my big toes—and then he looked away, his gaze falling to his own feet, and all I could think was look at me again, please.

"Of course?" he said.

I was nervous asking him, but it was the sensible thing to do if I was going to try and help get him out. He could be a murderer for all I knew. Or worse. I wasn't sure what could be worse than a murderer, but whatever it was, he could be it.

"Why did she do it? Why are you here?" My voice didn't sound like mine when I asked. It sounded far away, foreign to my ears. Like I was lying to myself that I didn't already know the answer. But I didn't.

He shook his head and looked back up at me. The second his eyes connected with mine, I felt bad that I had asked. Because he seemed angry again. The softness I had seen on his face was gone. His expression turned ugly and I leaned back out of self-preservation. Because right then, he scared me.

"I'm sorry, I didn't mean to upset you. I don't know you, though. You could be anyone!" My words came out in a rush and he laughed bitterly.

"No, you don't know me, do you?" He shook his head but held my gaze. "You want to know why Violet imprisoned me here?"

I nodded fractionally and tried to swallow around the lump in my throat.

"You want to know why I can't leave? Why I've been trapped here for ten goddamned years, without eating or drinking or sleeping, or feeling the wind on my skin or the cold rain on my face, or the heat of a woman's body on mine?"

He was even angrier now, and I was even more afraid. Afraid of what had made him this enraged and of the answer he was about to give me.

"Your grandmother trapped me here, in this godforsaken house in the middle of fucking nowhere—" He paused, his hands going to his hair and gripping it. He squeezed his eyes closed tightly, his lips pursed even tighter. He seemed to be to trying to control himself. Deep breaths. One. Two. Three. Finally he opened his eyes and looked at me again. "She was evil, and she was afraid of the future—of change."

He stood up, and his anger was palpable in the air between us, and I could admit that I was glad for the spell that made it impossible for him to touch me. Because the look on his face truly frightened me.

"I fell in love with the wrong woman, Sarah, so Violet trapped me here to keep me away from her, forever."

His words fell between us. Tired. Hopeless. Defeated.

My heart squeezed painfully and I struggled to breath.

He had loved the wrong woman? Why would Grandmother care about who Peter loved?

And why did I feel a prickle of jealousy at his admission?

Get a grip, Sarah! I chastised myself.

Peter paced the room, his breathing erratic. He ground his teeth together and I could feel my magic pinching at my fingertips again as my anxiety rose and fell with my breath.

Peter saw my magic burning and he stormed toward me, his face coming barely an inch from mine. He was trying to intimidate me, but I held my ground and refused to look away and show him how much he frightened me. His erratic emotions were giving me whiplash.

"You want to use your magic on me, Sarah?" he demanded, but I didn't reply. I didn't need to. It was right there, glowing from my fingertips. We could both sense my magic building. "Your magic is no good here—not for this. Only one witch rules this place, and she's dead. So take your false pity and your empty promises and forget about me." He stood up, his anger palpable but his shoulders sagging in defeat. "It's all just so hopeless, Sarah." He sounded pained and he gripped his hair.

The fire left him just as quickly as it came. And though his eyes flashed with a thousand apologies, they remained unsaid. Instead he turned and stormed out of the room.

I wanted to chase after him, but I didn't, because I couldn't. I turned and looked back at the spell book, thinking over what Peter had just said about my magic not being any good here. And he was right. At least for this particular spell.

Grandmother had spelled her book so no one could see inside of it. She wanted to hide something. Just like she had hidden Peter.

"Peter!" I yelled as I stood up, my heart racing.

He didn't come back. Of course he didn't.

I left Grandmother's bedroom and went in search of him. Because I knew how I could do it; I knew how I could set him free.

# *C*hapter *E*ight

I searched every inch of the house, but still didn't find Peter. So I decided that he either vanished to some secret half ghost place that I couldn't see whenever he felt like it, or he was purposefully hiding from me somewhere in this house, meaning he didn't want to be found.

Both options irritated me.

I didn't know why he would be angry with me. It wasn't my fault. I hadn't put him in this situation. And truthfully, I had my own life-threatening problems at the moment and didn't have the emotionally energy to invest in his issues.

But I had a plan. A plan, which could help us both.

Though Peter was being a typical man. He was rude and stubborn and hostile. And mostly he was just plain angry. So until he decided to make himself known, I couldn't tell him what my plan to help him was.

I slept once more on the sofa, and woke with a sore back. After a long shower and washing my hair three times, I still didn't feel clean. If I was being honest, it was a mental uncleanliness. Because the burden of grief felt heavier that day. I had so many questions for my grandmother, a woman who had practically raised me. But I would never be able to ask her now.

The water was as hot as I could stand it, until my skin turned red and tingled from the heat, yet it still didn't seem hot enough. I finally turned it off, standing there for a moment while I collected my emotions from the bottom of the shower stall before they drained away. I willed myself not to cry.

The water dripped from the ends of my hair and trailed down my body, and yet I still did not move. It was only when a chill formed on my skin and the humidity began to disperse so much that my teeth began to chatter that I grabbed the shower curtain and pulled it open.

A scream exploded out of me as Peter's dark gaze met mine. I gripped the damp shower curtain and wrapped it around me. His eyes raked over my partially covered body. A sly grin crept over his face, yet he thankfully averted his gaze.

"I'm sorry, I didn't mean to frighten you."

"Get out!" I gripped the curtain harder, and he chuckled and turned around.

I waited a moment to make sure that he wouldn't turn back around before I reached for the towel on the rack.

I wrapped the towel around myself and stepped out of the cubicle. "You don't just walk in on someone showering." A shiver worked its way up my spine as I stormed past him.

...It was like feather-light fingers dancing over my flesh. The kiss of touch, the breath of something true and here... I stopped in the doorway. I couldn't feel him, and he couldn't feel me, and yet...

"Did you feel that?" he asked sharply, drawing me up short. He pinned me to the doorframe with his stare, his body close to mine.

I nodded, my breathing heavy. "I felt something..."

I wasn't certain what I had felt. It could have been a draft. A sudden gust of wind. But of course, I chastised myself, it could have been him. His touch.

His eyes were frantic for a moment. "I felt my face, yesterday," he murmured as he reached with hesitant fingers towards his skin. His nose. His cheeks. He frowned, and I knew that whatever he had experienced before was gone now. And he was frustrated and sad. "I felt my beard for the first time in ten years, and then it just...went."

He shook his head, as though trying to clear his thoughts.

"But that," he swallowed, "that was something different. It was hot and cold, a shiver of ice and the blanket of warmth. It was something…"

"…and yet nothing…" I finished for him, trying to pretend it wasn't anything purposeful. Though for his sake or mine, I wasn't sure. Because with that one touch, a flutter started in my heart.

The flash of lips on skin. Of hands on hips. Of warm brown eyes staring into mine.

"It was everything," he breathed, sounding desperate. The gap between us was minute—so close, in fact, that I would have felt the heat coming from his body…if he were really there.

I couldn't imagine what it was like to exist in this in-between state, not being able to feel. To hardly be alive. He may have been moody and at times cruel. He was hard to read and sometimes even harder to like, but on some level I understood him. He was trapped. Just like me. He craved freedom and it had changed him on a fundamental level. Being a prisoner changed everyone. Including myself.

There was a brief moment of empathy that flashed between us. That connection that thrummed between us strengthened and seemed to be pulling us together. I took a tentative step forward, almost as though my feet moved of their own volition. It wasn't a conscious thought, but a necessary movement I couldn't resist.

If I reached out my hand and put my fingers on the side of his neck, right where the pulse thumped beneath barely there skin, would he feel it? What would happen?

I wanted to find out.

I lifted my hand as I moved toward him. Peter watched me, his eyes growing wider. Apprehensive. Needy. He wanted it too. Maybe more than I did.

"You should get ready," he said suddenly, a little too loudly, taking a decisive step backwards, and I hastily dropped my hand to my side while my other continued to clutch the towel around my body. Because I was still half naked with wet hair and zero makeup. Just great.

"That's probably a good idea. I don't want to hang out in a towel all day," I joked, trying to laugh, but it sounded brittle and false.

Peter's eyes heated briefly and I felt myself flush under the intensity of his gaze. My mouth went suddenly dry and my stomach twisted deliciously.

Peter looked away from me and I felt cold. From the inside out. The loss of his eyes left me feeling strangely bereft. Which was crazy. I needed to get myself together and stop getting lost in irrational delusions about the phantom guy hanging out in my bathroom.

"I'll be downstairs waiting for you," he said, his voice clipped and cold. Then he turned, without looking at me again, and left.

I turned back to my reflection and realized that I was smiling. I couldn't remember the last time I'd smiled like that. A full-toothed grin that I felt in my cheeks. I touched my lips, feeling a change deep inside me.

I was smiling.

I was happy.

Here in this cursed home with the fear of my coven looming large, I felt something like contentment.

I ran my fingers through my hair, feeling my heart swell with something I had never felt before, and it was both frightening and exciting—something I couldn't quite identify, but it was there all the same. I brushed my teeth. I combed my hair and put it in a quick braid. I applied minimal makeup. And when I was finished, I liked the look of the woman in the mirror. She was pretty. Flushed and dewy from her shower. And there was a sparkle in her eyes that was good to see. It was me, but a different version of me.

I went to my bedroom and got dressed, putting on a pair of old blue jeans and a long-sleeved tee—something comfortable but cute. It was the first time in days that I felt like putting forth any effort. I didn't want to examine too closely where the change had come from. But I knew, deep down, that it had everything to do with the man downstairs.

After coming downstairs, I found Peter standing by the living room window looking out into the forest. He didn't turn at the sound of me, though I could tell that he heard me. His arms were folded across his broad chest, and his fingers were drumming a beat on his arm.

I wondered what that must feel like—to move but to not feel it.

"They're out there, you know. They're waiting for you," he said, looking at something I couldn't see.

"I know," I said softly, moving to stand beside him.

"What do you think they will do to you?" he asked, his voice hard.

I tensed. Was he being cruel or was he genuinely curious? Maybe he was worried. I couldn't tell. But I sort of hoped it was the latter.

He finally turned to look at me, his mouth pressed into a thin line and his eyes looking soulful.

"I'm not sure," I said, hesitantly.

I turned my back on him and walked to the kitchen. I wasn't going to stand there and ponder my ultimate demise. I couldn't. My palms were itching again, my fingers fizzed with magic. I wanted to destroy things. To hurt people. It was there, buried just below the surface, begging to be let out.

I gripped the edge of the kitchen sink and tried to calm myself down. I gazed into the white porcelain, at the lines and cracks and deep imperfection in the smooth surface. I stared and I breathed calmly, feeling equal parts hurt and rage in my chest.

"Your mother hated you, Sarah."

I hadn't heard him follow me but I should have expected it.

Part of me hated him, this total stranger, for spitting out the truth that I loathed to admit, even to myself. Part of me detested his casual cruelty and lackadaisical viciousness. He tore me down so easily. But whenever I looked into his face, I saw something other than his anger. I saw something beyond his bitterness. Just beyond my reach.

I wasn't sure what it was. Maybe it was the flicker of something deeper in his eyes. Maybe it was the way he watched me, trying to hide the pain. But I knew. He didn't want to say those things. Yet for some reason he felt he needed to.

"I listened to Violet and your mother talk about you. Before you left and afterwards. They argued a lot. But that woman, she hated you. That was obvious."

I gritted my teeth and turned to face him, refusing to hide my face. I wouldn't let him see how much he bothered me. "I don't care," I lied.

He watched me through soft eyes that saw right through to my soul. "Yes, you do." He spoke bluntly, calmly. "You always cared."

I hated it. It didn't feel real. I hated the illusion of hate he exuded. It infuriated me. I wanted the warmth that he was trying to conceal. I craved it.

We stood in silence, the sun warm on my back, and I wanted to tell him how good it felt, but I didn't. Because, unlike him, I didn't want to continue this cycle of misery. I was not like my mother or the rest of my coven. And I wouldn't be like him either—maiming with words when I wanted something else entirely. So I remained quiet and looked away.

"Your mother will kill you to take your power. You know that, don't you?" Once again he spoke bluntly and without feeling, his casual talk of my demise cutting through me like a knife.

"Then let her try." I lifted my chin in defiance, my spine straight and strong.

"You should be scared. You should leave," he continued harshly, sounding frustrated. "You should leave right now."

"I'm scared. I'm not going to lie. But I'm not going to hide either," I told him, sounding confident, even if I didn't really feel it.

I heard him let out an irritated sigh. "You're stubborn. I had forgotten how much." His hand raked over his jaw, rubbing to soothe his irritation but feeling nothing.

"What?" I asked, surprised, turning to look at him again. I was even more shocked to find him smiling. The sort of smile that warmed my heart and made me feel things that I shouldn't.

Peter lifted his eyes and looked at me and I found it hard to breathe. So many things went unsaid. So many things that he seemed unwilling to share.

"What do you mean, you'd forgotten how much?" I demanded.

*The faintest memory of hands on my face. Lips on mine, and kisses that I wanted to last forever...*

He looked away, a frown on his face. "I've been here a long time, remember? I've been an audience to your bullheadedness many times before," he explained roughly, and I felt a crushing sense of disappointment.

Why? What did I think he meant?

"I think I can help you," I said, trying to shake off the strange feeling of déjà vu.

Peter bit down on his bottom lip and I tried not to stare at his mouth. "No one can help me," he said despairingly.

"Well, I think I can." I stood up straight. I wouldn't let him see my doubt. I wouldn't let him witness a failure.

Peter frowned. "You couldn't see her spells, remember? Don't give me false hope. Not from you."

"Just listen for a minute—"

"Don't. Just don't, Sarah." He looked so, so angry.

"I think, when she is buried—" I continued, not letting him deter me.

"Stop it." He shook his head in agitation. "Just stop it!" Agony. So much agony. But he just needed to listen to me.

"Her magic will go back to the coven—"

"No more, Sarah!"

"And some of that magic will return to me."

"I said stop it, Sarah!" he roared and I flinched. Even though I knew on some level that he would never hurt me, I couldn't help but recoil in the face of his fury.

When he saw the look on my face, something flickered in his eyes and he took a step backwards, giving us both some distance that we needed.

"But don't you see? I'll be as powerful as she ever was," I whispered, scared to raise my voice. "I will have her magic!" I lifted my hands, reaching for him. He leaned in slightly. We were close. So close.

The air hummed between us and my heart slammed against my ribcage. We were both breathing heavily and I still hadn't touched him. My fingers curled in mid-air...waiting.

"I'm scared that it won't be enough. That I'll break all over again," he choked out and I saw it. The moment he shattered.

And I felt his pain as if it resided in my own heart.

I felt his anger bubbling in my veins.

And his grief...

Good God, his grief would suffocate me.

A tear slipped down my cheek, and I watched his eyes follow its slow descent.

Slowly, my hand touched his face and I gasped. I could feel him. His warm, soft skin felt alive under my fingers. His pupils dilated, and he let out a soft moan from trembling lips.

"I can feel you," I said in wonder, running my hand down the length of his cheek. "I can feel you!" I repeated, elated.

"Sarah." He said my name like a promise, like a declaration of something powerful and beautiful. He put his hand over mine and held it against his face, his eyes closing. "Sarah," he whispered. A chant. A prayer. I clung to that one word as he gripped my hand, kissing my knuckles over and over.

His lips warm. His breath hot.

"Sarah." He murmured again.

It was the most wonderful word in the world—my name on this man's lips. I felt it in every part of my body. It caressed me like I imagined his fingers would. As though he were making love to me with his voice.

Just by saying my name.

I didn't dare look away, in case the moment was lost forever, for him and for me.

These feeling—these feelings! They were new and old all at once. Like I had experienced them a time before. They assaulted my senses, stroking along the curve of my spine and down into the chasms of my heart.

His breathing was as erratic as mine, chests rising and falling. The *thump thump thump* of our hearts beating as we pleaded with ourselves, with each other, for this to be real. To last.

I could feel and he could feel, and we were feeling together, and it was truly magical.

He closed the small gap between us, almost hesitantly, pressing his chest against mine, and then he groaned loudly when our bodies made contact. His hands released my hands and moved to my wrists, *up up up* across my arms and elbows, up to my shoulders and neck, and then his hands were fisting my hair and tilting my mouth up to meet his, and he was pressing all of himself against me.

It was reckless and scary. I was submitting to someone…to something I didn't understand.

I knew, in part, that he wasn't talking to me anymore, and I was okay with that. I wanted to be his fountain of cold water in an arid desert.

"Sarah." He said my name again like he was asking permission, and I nodded, both equally wanting and needing more of him. It was more than just desire and need inside me, because everything was just so much more right now. It was like he owned me—every curve was his, and every inch of soft skin belonged to him. He owned my body and he owned my mind, and though that should have frightened me, it didn't. I felt like it was exactly how it was supposed to be.

Like we were always meant to be.

As I thought it, his touch began to vanish. The graze of his fingers became lighter until it was nothing. He staggered backwards, gasping for air, his eyes frantically locked on mine.

I clasped a hand over my mouth, willing the tears not to come. So much pain. That was all I could see in his eyes, in his face and his shaking hands and trembling body. The quake of fear and sadness engulfing him, swallowing the man whole.

He had lived with that suffering—that torment—for so long that the fear of nothingness was drowning him, stealing the very core of who he really was. A touch to him was everything. It was his air. It was his nourishment. It was life. And to have it snatched away after only a brief touch of it was killing him.

Whatever spell he was under, I needed to break it soon, because it wouldn't be long before all that he was—who he was before all of this happened—would be lost forever to that misery.

I knew that he would never be the same again.

Who he was, who he really was, was dying inside of him.

I didn't know how he'd survived so long… just a moment of his touch, and now, to be without it... I already felt like I was wasting away inside. I wasn't sure if I'd just made his pain worse or more bearable, but the guilt was eating away at me as he closed his eyes and held a fist to his chest like he wanted to hammer away the pain.

When his lids opened, he stared at the floor, the hard creases of sadness and frustration showering his face like a thousand wretched kisses.

"Are you okay?" I asked, my voice shaking with each word. I was afraid he was about to break, to crumble to nothing. And then he looked up at me and he smiled.

"That was worth the wait." He said softly.

I frowned, unsure what he meant, but my thoughts were interrupted as a squawk sounded outside the kitchen window. Peter's gaze lifted from the floor to behind me. His beautiful face turned at once angry. I wanted to say sorry, to apologize again and again to him, but it would make no difference.

I turned around slowly to face the flock of ravens outside of the window. They swooped through the air, diving at the window before lifting higher seconds before they hit and broke the glass. I flinched every time, hating myself for flinching, for being fearful that my spell may not have been strong enough and they might get in. But mostly I hated myself for caring that one of them might get hurt.

"They're just trying to frighten you," Peter said, though I wasn't sure he believed it.

I glanced sideways at him, seeing that he was watching me, and I nodded in agreement.

"You protected yourself?" he asked.

"Yes, and the house." I nodded. "They can't get in here."

"Then don't fear them, Sarah. They can't hurt you."

Why did his words feel like lies, no matter how much I wanted to trust them?

"They can't hurt you anymore," he murmured, his face turning away from me to look outside.

I did the same, looked away from him, toward the birds that still swooped through the sky, and I continued to flinch regardless. "Not today, at least," I murmured.

# *Chapter Nine*

The ravens swooped for over an hour before perching upon the overlooking trees. They watched me as I watched them. It was a standoff, but one I gave up on after a while. This wasn't, after all, the battle I needed to win.

"You should drink something."

I looked up at Peter with a frown. "What?"

He scratched his chin, or tried to. His eyes were deep and open, like ravines. "Tea, coffee." He shrugged nonchalantly. "You're shaking—a hot drink will help." He stopped scratching at his nonexistent beard and pointed to my hands.

I looked down, seeing that yes, I was in fact shaking—a soft tremble to my hands from the anxiety of the morning and the power still itching at my palms. I nodded and turned toward the kettle, setting it to boil. I glanced up, seeing the ravens that were still there, and I abruptly reached over and closed the curtains, plunging the kitchen into darkness.

I rubbed my fingertips together, and when that didn't work I rubbed my palms together. The friction felt good, like scratching an itch I had not been able to reach in a long time. I closed my eyes and let the vibrations take away the ache inside me as I steadied myself and my magic.

The kettle began to whistle loudly, and I opened my eyes and made myself a black coffee before moving to the living room and sitting on the sofa. Peter trailed after me, moving to stand by the window to keep watch.

"Are they still out there?" I asked.

"Yes," he said simply. "They're not doing anything now."

I watched him. He was facing away from me with his arms crossed, his muscles hard and tense, and I wondered if he would say something cruel to me again. I hoped not, because I didn't have the energy to take any more hurt. Not from him, not from anyone. I wasn't sure what had just happened between us in the kitchen, but I could feel something growing inside of me. Something that he brought to life. I wanted more of it, but his touches were few and far between, and his mood shifts were violent and unpredictable.

Yet he knew more than he was letting on—of that I was certain.

Despite his cruelty toward me sometimes, he cared for me. That much was obvious. And it was obvious that his cruelty hurt not just me, but him. Though I hardly knew him, I knew that there was a deeper connection between us than I understood.

"Will you tell me what's going on?" I asked, deciding to be as simple and direct as he was.

For several moments he didn't move, and then slowly turned to face me. He looked hesitant and uncomfortable. "I can't."

"Why?" My coffee mug was hot in my hands, but right then I relished the burn of it against my palms.

He swallowed and looked away. "Because it doesn't matter. None of it matters."

"Do I know you? Did I know you? Before…?" I was hesitant, unsure of what I was saying because I had no memory of him, and yet there was a familiarity with him that sang to my soul.

"It doesn't matter." He said it like a plea, and this time he didn't get angry.

"I don't understand." I shook my head and stood up. "Please, Peter, help me to understand." I took a step toward him, expecting him to move, but he didn't. He stayed where he was, frozen to the spot, watching me. "When I get her magic, I'll get you out of here. I promise." I took another step forward.

"I don't think you should." He replied.

"Don't say that!" I yelled, my voice rising and taking him by surprise.

"You just need to leave, Sarah. Can't you see how much danger you're in?"

"Stop it. Please, stop it," I begged, feeling angry and sad and confused. "I feel...connected to you, Peter. I don't know why, and I don't understand it, but I feel it all the same."

"I can't protect you, Sarah," he replied coldly, looking away. "And I'll never be free."

I knew it hurt him to say those words; I knew that because it hurt me. Like a stab to the gut, I felt like he had cut me, sliced me open and left me bleeding and raw. I wanted to yell at him, to make him tell me what the hell was going on. I didn't even know that I wanted to be with him. Not after the many times that he'd hurt me. Yet him saying that we couldn't be together made me feel something that I didn't understand.

"I can protect myself." I replied calmly, though my hands shook.

He looked back at me finally and scoffed at my suggestion.

"I can." I snapped, feeling angry. "I don't need you to protect me, I just need..."

I didn't really know what I needed, or what I was suggesting. I just knew I couldn't stand the thought of leaving here and never seeing this man again. It was ridiculous. I felt nothing for him, yet I wanted him in my life.

"We can never be together." He said coldly.

Why not? I cried out, feeling a tsunami of emotions colliding into me.

"If we are together, it will kill you." He replied to my unspoken question.

I stared at him even more confused, knowing that I was finally getting some truth from him.

"And it will kill me." Peter took a step forward, closing the small gap until we were almost touching. But the magic that had worked for us before was now working against us, because I couldn't feel him when he reached for me. He took a deep breath before speaking, as if the words were a heavy burden, and I braced myself for what he would say. "Sarah, if we are together, we will destroy everyone. And so I'll never be free, because even if I'm not here, in this house, I will always be chained to you. I will…" he stopped himself from finishing his sentence, and I was glad, because I feared what he would say next.

With one last sorrowful look, he walked away from me. And I let him.

I stared silently into the fire as dawn approached. Peter had walked away from me the night before, leaving me without hope and filled with even more questions.

He never returned, instead leaving me to myself. I hated it, and yet I was grateful for it. I hadn't had a moment to myself since I had arrived back, and the silence allowed me to process.

I was tired. The previous night I had begun practicing magic. The itch and burn in my palms had begun to get too much for me to take. Besides, I needed to practice before the funeral, just in case.

I hoped that Mother would understand my need to say goodbye, and would let me do so in peace. I had wanted nothing more to do with the coven and its magic—at least before I met Peter. Now I needed just a little of Grandmother's magic to save him. Mother was welcome to the title of coven leader—she could have everything—but I had to participate in the ritual to receive my inheritance: a portion of my grandmother's magic. I would never forgive myself if I didn't. Despite what Peter had said.

The day was not going to be a good one. It would be all about goodbyes and confrontation—two things that I hugely despised

But that day I needed to be strong, stronger than I had ever been, because any amount of weakness would set my mother off on a rampage. A rampage which I knew was surely coming and was inevitable, yet I still wanted to put it off for as long as I could.

I finally looked away from the flames and made my way upstairs. I showered, letting the water wash over me for the longest time.

I knew I was trying to prolong the morning, to extend my solitude until the inevitable. And I knew why. It was not just that I didn't want to go to Grandmother's funeral and face my coven's wrath. I knew that it was because, at some point that day, when Grandmother was put back into the earth, her magic would soak into me and I would have the power to see her spells in her magic book, and then I would have the power to release Peter. I wanted to help Peter, I really did. Even though he had been hateful and cruel, I could understand his bitterness. He was a prisoner and no one deserved that fate, no matter how cantankerous.

But I could also admit that a small part of me didn't want to see him go. Despite his attitude, I couldn't deny the connection between us. When we had touched the day before, I had felt something deep and pure that I hadn't been expecting. It was confusing. It made my heart ache but I wanted to feel it again.

And so, I would go back to the coven for as long as it would take to bury my grandmother. I would wear my coven's traditional brooch in secret. The brooch would be the only way to channel the power that was mine by birthright. Without it, I'd never be able to take what was mine, which I desperately needed to help Peter.

The other witches would know what I had done once the magic began to flow to us all, but hopefully it would be too late for them to stop me.

Being surreptitious was paramount. Because if my mother saw me wearing the brooch, she would surely kill me.

My actions would be seen as a threat to her power. She would never understand that I wanted nothing to do with the coven. With the title. With the power. All I wanted was to help Peter. I had made a promise and I would keep it.

I dressed in a simple black dress and shoes. I tied my hair into a ponytail and put on minimal makeup. Then I went to retrieve the brooch.

I hesitated for several minutes, clasping it in the palm of my hand and trying to decide where to pin it so that no one would see. In the end, I pinned it over my heart and then put a black shawl over the top of it. I knew it was there, the magic vibrated through my skin. But no one but me would know I wore it.

I didn't see Peter when I went downstairs. I wasn't sure where he was, but I had a feeling he was avoiding me.

I should have been offended—hurt, even. I was risking everything to help him and he couldn't even see me off to my grandmother's funeral.

But I knew there was more going on with him and I would eventually find out all of his secrets. Because I knew, somehow, they were important for both of us.

"I'll set you free, Peter, I promise," I said, looking around the empty room. The only reply was the wind whistling at the windows.

So I left, feeling hope that I needed to believe in.

## Chapter Ten

Peter.

**"I**'ll set you free, Peter, I promise." The words floated in the air, hitting me right in the heart.

I wanted to tell her not to. To forget about me. But I knew she wouldn't…she couldn't. Her feelings for me, while confusing and maybe a little convoluted, were starting to return. I knew I was making it harder by being hateful and then touching her. But where Sarah was concerned, I had never been rational. I knew that forgetting me was the best thing for her.

But having her remember was the best thing for me.

My love for her beat against my chest and threatened to explode out of me. It was wild. Unrestrained. And desperate for her.

But to love me would be her undoing. And I didn't want my freedom at the cost of her life.

I sat down on the floor, my back against the back door of the kitchen, and I wondered if I was really the selfish man that Violet had said I was.

Our love would kill us both. It was insanity, but it was the truth. We were anomalies and we went against our very nature, but now that she was here again I was terrified I'd never be able to let her go. Even if it meant the death of everything.

Memories of Sarah and I came to the surface. The more I tried to push them away, the more they fought for substance.

We had been children when we first met, and even then, at such a young age, we both knew that together we would be something special. Unfortunately, so did Violet. As the years passed, we found ways to see each other, meeting in secret. It was always platonic, always just friendship, until one day it wasn't.

\*

*"She almost caught me." Sarah laughed, her hand finding mine. She twined her fingers with mine and I smiled as we ran.*

*"Why can't they just leave us alone?" I grumbled, feeling angry.*

*These days I was always feeling angry. Where Sarah was light, I seemed to be the dark.*

*She glanced across at me, sensing my anger, and she gave my hand a small squeeze in comfort. "It doesn't matter. They can't keep us apart no matter what they do." She let out another laugh, and this time I felt myself laughing with her.*

*We finally stopped for breath. We were at the far end of the forest and across the shallow stream now—far enough away that we could both take a moment to rest. Sarah let go of my hand and I bent over, hands on my knees, to catch my breath, still chuckling. Because yes, they couldn't keep us apart. No matter how hard they tried.*

*"I like that."*

*I looked up. "What?"*

*"Your laugh. You don't do it enough." She smiled, and I looked away flustered.*

*It was true. She was the only one who could ever make me smile or laugh. My heart felt dark and heavy, not pure like the rest of my coven. That worried me. Yet when I was with Sarah, all my troubles drifted away, because nothing and no one mattered but her.*

*"I do when I'm with you," I stated, standing full upright.*

*I was tall now, my shoulders growing wider, my muscles defining. I was at that moment between man and boy. That transition where everything seems so muddled and yet so crystal clear. I watched Sarah as she reached down and plucked a flower from the ground, twirling it between her slender fingers. She looked at me through her dark lashes and smiled again.*

*"Yes you do," she replied, taking a step backwards. "Come on, let's keep going." She turned swiftly, her dress skimming around her thighs.*

*Her step faltered as she stumbled over a broken tree limb and fell to the ground, landing awkwardly. I moved to her swiftly, kneeling down to help her back up.*

*"Are you okay?"*

*She took my hand and climbed to her knees with another laugh. "Just clumsy."*

*I smiled again, relishing in the warmth of her hand in mine. "You should be more careful," I teased.*

*"You should be more alert to stop me from tripping," she teased back.*

*I laughed, and she beamed at me.*

*"I love that sound."*

*"So you said," I replied, taking her other hand.*

*Her eyes were the darkest of brown, swallowing me up. I let out a slow breath, the world seeming to come to a stop around us as we stared into one another's eyes. I wasn't laughing anymore, and I wasn't smiling. I was feeling something altogether different. And by the way she was looking at me, she was feeling it too. A strange feeling of belonging, of coming home, of being exactly where I should be in life.*

*My feelings for her had been growing for a while, morphing into something more than friendship. Something unexplainable. Yet whatever it was, it felt right.*

*"Sarah." I whispered her name. When she didn't say anything in return I reached over, my hand tentatively cupping her left cheek. Her eyes locked with mine, her lips parting slightly, and then I leaned forward and pressed my lips to hers.*

*I waited a beat, expecting her to pull away, to tease me and laugh. But she didn't. Instead her own hands came up to my shoulders and pulled me closer. And then I let myself finally fall into her.*

\*

I'm not sure how long I stayed there; time passes differently for me than it does for others. I didn't sleep, but I closed my eyes and I daydreamed about things. I saw what my life might have been like if I had never met Violet, if I had never fallen in love with Sarah that day so long ago.

Perhaps I would have become the next leader of my coven after my father, as I was always intended to be. I was a powerful witch, even if I had always felt out of place.

Maybe I would have left everything and traveled the world. I had always dreamt of climbing mountains and sailing oceans. I had always yearned for more than my coven and my pre-destined life.

Dreams, hopes, fantasies—they were all gone.

I felt like sobbing. It would be wonderful to let down my guard long enough to allow myself tears, but I couldn't. Ten years I had been there, watching, waiting, and hoping.

Sometimes I could pretend that my hatred for Sarah was real. After all, she was the reason I was a prisoner. I would become so despondent that I longed for the black bitterness to take over everything. My imprisonment would be easier to bear if I didn't love her so damn much.

But I couldn't. Hating Sarah was an impossibility. I could no more make myself hate her than I could stop myself from loving her. Because this was all my own damn fault for falling in love with someone that I wasn't supposed to.

But how do you not fall in love with someone?

How do you tell your heart that it can't ever have its other half? Or that it will always feel empty and painful because you can never be with your soul mate?

I didn't know why I hadn't told Sarah the truth—all of it. Why I was trapped. Our passionate but doomed history.

Perhaps the truth was just too painful. So, yeah, your grandmother trapped me here because I fell in love with you. Because apparently if we were ever to be together, our love would destroy everything because our magic just isn't compatible. It definitely sucks.

Because that was the root of our problem. The reason we were never going to be together. Why it was so wrong, for everyone, that we had wanted each other so much.

I was light.

Sarah was dark.

To fuse our magic together would destroy everything. Our covens. The very fabric of the world we lived in. And of course, each other.

Our love was wrong. It was against our very natures. So why had it been allowed to exist in the first place?

My coven and Sarah's coven were mortal enemies. We grew up believing very different things, learning very different magic, yet in some ways we were so much alike.

Sarah and I were both the grandchildren of our highest leaders. We were powerful but we were uncontrollable. We both craved the power that bubbled inside us. If we ever were to be together, the power that we shared would destroy everything.

I stood back up, feeling mentally and physically exhausted. I wanted to vanish into nothing; it was the only way to end this pain, to stop my heart from aching like it did. Sarah and I were never meant to be together. Yet our love had been a gift. After centuries of hate, we could re-write our covens' story. We could have started something new. Something different. We had truly believed that our love could do great things.

But that wasn't how our story ended up.

We were powerful. And if we were to be together, our covens would be blown apart.

Everything we knew, everything we had ever been, would be over.

But there was a piece to this puzzle that I was missing—something more to all this than I knew. But I didn't know that I necessarily wanted to learn it. What purpose would it serve? What would it change? Sarah and I couldn't be together and that was all that I needed to know.

I had spent so long being angry at Violet for punishing me. Angry at Sarah for not being strong enough to remember me, and for agreeing to leave. But maybe Violet had been right in keeping Sarah and I apart. Because the longer she was here, the harder it was for me to stay away from her. To deny my love for her.

A love that I knew would kill us both.

Because I worried that even the strongest magic couldn't keep us apart.

# Chapter Eleven

## Sarah

The drive to Grandmother's funeral was unnerving. I couldn't stop thinking about Peter the entire time. Touching him had awakened something inside of me that I hadn't realized had been lying dormant. Despite the rollercoaster of emotions I had been on since I had come back to Raven's Cove, I felt strangely at peace with Peter. It made no sense but I felt it all the same.

I noticed that I was followed the entire way to the funeral by a flock of ravens. When I stopped at intersections or lights, they stopped too—perching on the telephone lines or nearby trees. And when I continued to drive, they took to the skies once again.

More birds joined the flock as I got closer, until I was attracting the attention of other people. Onlookers pointed at the sky, staring slack-jawed at the mass of birds circling my car.

I was afraid, but I refused to let that stop me from doing what I had come to do.

As I pulled into the cemetery and past the main gates, the ravens flew on ahead of me and I could finally take a breath.

I had to do this, I knew I had to, and any reservations I had about attending the funeral had been completely blown away by making my promise to Peter, but that didn't mean I wasn't worried.

I pulled into a parking space in front of the small brick building and shut off the engine. Family, friends, and strangers were heading inside, all of them dressed head to toe in black, and all of them wearing their brooches. I knew that most of them were there only to receive their portion of my grandmother's magic, and not because they loved the woman in any way. It was all about power.

In the five years since I had been banished, I had never stopped missing home or missing her. My grandmother. The magic that lived inside me was a constant reminder of what I had been forced to give up, but as the years passed I'd felt the light begin to filter back into my bloodstream and the darkness ebb away. I still missed her, but I would always want the light rather than the dark, and if that meant losing my family, then so be it. Until now...until Peter.

I tightened my shawl around my shoulders and got out of my jeep. The second I did, the witches that were making their way into the coven church stopped dead in their tracks and turned to face me.

Our coven's church was a small, beautiful building nestled deep within the forest. It was said to be over four hundred years old, and yet it still held a newness to it as if it had just been built. Colorful stained glass windows on either side contrasted against the grey stone walls of the building, and two tall wooden doors held the only opening.

The other witches backed away as I walked toward the entrance. I felt them follow closely behind as I made my way inside. I wasn't sure if it was to keep an eye on me, to intimidate me, or to be close on hand should any drama start—though I was pretty sure it was a little bit of all three.

People turned in their seats as I made my way down the center of the aisle toward the pew at the very front, where Grandmother's closest family was supposed to sit. The church was not in the traditional Christian sense. It was a building used by the covens for important events. In many ways it resembled any other religious structure with stained glass, pews, and an elaborate altar at the front. But that's where the similarities ended. Instead of the symbols of traditional faiths, the tools of a witch's coven were on hand. The athame. The chalice. And of course the pentacle, representing the magic that coursed through all of our veins.

The High Priest greeted me with a slow nod of his head. It was noncommittal and nonjudgmental, and I was grateful for it.

Grandmother's coffin was in front of the altar, and I went and joined the line that had formed of those who wished to pay their respects.

It wasn't long before I was standing in front of her open casket, looking down on her face. It was eerie, staring at her lifeless body. She didn't appear to be dead. She looked as though she were sleeping peacefully.

Violet hadn't changed in any way. Her hair was still long and dark, braided over one shoulder, as she always wore it. Her lashes were thick and dark on her pale cheeks, and her lips were a deep, vibrant red.

I took comfort in the familiarity of her face—how, even in death, she was still just as remarkable as she had been in life. Grandmother's magic had always kept her young and beautiful, so even in death she was stunning.

I wished I could have asked her about Peter.

Perhaps there was another reason for imprisoning him—one that would make more sense. But I couldn't ask her, so her cruelty to him was the only blemish I saw on her perfect face.

I loved her and yet I was angry with her. It was the usual dichotomy of our relationship. Some things would never change. Even with her passing.

"Sarah."

My heart stuttered at the sound of her voice.

Mother.

I turned to look at her, and she, just like Grandmother, hadn't changed in the time I had been away. I gave her a curt nod—a simple sign of respect that I hoped would go a long way toward appeasing her. I could tell almost immediately that it hadn't worked.

"Mother," I said shortly and turned away, hoping to avoid a confrontation.

I took my seat next to one of my many cousins. My mother made no attempt to talk to me, or even to acknowledge me, so I chose to do the same. My mother leaned down to kiss Grandmother on her cheek, and then she stood back up. As she turned and walked back to her seat, her eyes sought me out and a slow, mean smile crept across her lips.

Her lips, like Grandmother's, were painted a fiery red. But that's where the similarities ended. Her eyes were cold where my grandmother's had only ever been warm.

I looked away and let my gaze fall back to the High Priest. He spoke about her love of baking and her famous remedies for blocked magic. He reminded the coven of how much she loved her fellow witches and her family. How she would do anything to protect them, and how we each played an important role in her life.

"And that now it's time for you to play an important role in her death," he continued solemnly. I stiffened, knowing what was coming.

"Through her and in her and with her, you will set her soul free and send her home. She becomes a direct line to our ancestors, and with her death we will make her magic our own. This is her gift to us." He smiled as her casket filled with a blue light "It's time," he said. "Will her daughters come forward, please?"

Mother and her two sisters made their way toward the High Priest. Each of them nodded at him. One by one they stood at a corner of her casket. Finally, he looked across the front two rows, seeking out the most powerful of nieces. His gaze landed on me and he swiftly moved on. He walked from one side of the line to the other

111

and then made his way up the steps before turning to face the coven once more.

"Sarah, please step forward and help lay your grandmother to eternal rest with the earth." He didn't look at me when he said it, and I was glad because he would have seen the shock on my face.

My eyes darted to Mother, but she was looking somewhere else, far away from me— her only daughter. She would hate me for this— I would hate me for this.

I stood at the remaining corner of the casket, and when the High Priest bowed his head, giving us his assent, we began to chant.

"Comereth, a'taleth du vineyas. Comereth, a'taleth du vineyas. Comereth, a'taleth du vineyas."

The casket began to lift as the rest of the coven started to filter back outside. I uttered the words, so unfamiliar to me, and yet words that as a witch, were etched into my mind. With our power we guided her casket down the center aisle of the church and outside into the daylight, the blue glow of her power hovering above her body.

We walked slowly, chanting in unison every step of the way as we passed through the grounds of the cemetery until finally we reached Grandmother's plot.

We lowered the coffin into the ground, and then we uttered a different chant. This one was louder. As our voices lifted into a cacophony of prayer and power, one by one the members of the coven transformed into ravens with black feathers and golden eyes. They lifted into the air, hovering above the open plot

As the last member became the raven, the coffin evaporated with a loud crack of splintering wood, leaving her body naked and bare to the earth.

The High Priest waved his hands over the ground and made it shudder and quake until the soil covered her naked form, embracing her once and for all.

We stopped chanting, and the witches turned back into their human forms before coming to stand in a circle around the mound of earth where she lay.

They each stepped forward and spat on her grave to acknowledge her passing and their grief for it. I took my turn, spitting on the mound of earth even as I doubted my own conviction, and then I stepped back, allowing another in my place.

When the final witch had expressed her sadness, the High Priest passed around a ceremonial bowl, and we each sliced a line across our palms and allowed our blood to drip

113

into the bowl. As the bowl began to fill with everyone's blood, the earth trembled beneath us. I could feel the soft vibrations beneath my feet, trembling up my legs. The feeling continued until the bowl was full and every witch had shared her blood.

The High Priest got down on his knees and poured our blood over the earth, marking her grave and offering up our bodies ready to take her magic. He whispered a small prayer, sacred words for only him and the earth to bear witness to.

After the final prayer had been uttered, he stood and turned to us. With a slow nod of his head he turned and left, as such, giving us his blessing to leave. Slowly we begin to filter out of the cemetery.

Now it was just a matter of time as we waited for her to pass her magic on to us.

I was glad that it was over and that she could be at peace, but the selfish part of me was still heartbroken and confused. I had so many questions left unasked. So many things that I needed to know.

I looked at my feet as I walked, eyes trained on the ground as I attempted to make my escape. I was almost to my Jeep when I heard her.

I froze, the blood that I had so freely bled for my grandmother freezing in my body.

"Sarah."

My mother was calling me.

The time had come.

# *Chapter Twelve*

Night fell quickly in the cemetery of Raven's Cove. With one quick swoop of a blanket, the world became dark and night enveloped us.

I turned to face my mother. After five years, the hatred she felt for me was still painted starkly on her familiar face.

"Are you leaving so soon?"

"Yes," I replied neutrally. I made sure to hide all other feelings she could use against me.

She raised an eyebrow at me, her mouth quirking into a sly smile. "Come, child, we have much to discuss."

She turned and began to walk away before I could refuse her, leaving me no other option but to follow. Four other coven members trailed after her, walking in her wake. I recognized them instantly. They were women that I had grown up with, witches I had called friends, and now they were her loyal followers.

Geneva, Maraud, Saskia, and Devine. Young and impressionable, and all committed to my mother's cause. They had always been that way. Even as children they had wanted to do someone's bidding; never content with having their own magic, they wanted to be guided, led into deeper and darker paths. And now they had their way, with my mother leading them.

Mother made her way into the forest behind the cemetery and I briefly looked back toward my jeep as I followed her. My means of escape was moving further and further away.

Everyone watched us, their faces closed and stony. There would be no help from any of them. I had known that's how it would be, but the betrayal still stung.

The forest thickened around me, but soon enough we come to a clearing and I could see my mother and her four friends waiting. I swallowed down the lump in my throat and stood my ground.

My fingers were positively burning with the need to expel magic, but I kept my hands closed into tight fists.

"What do you want, Mother?" I asked, choosing to be direct.

"What are you doing back here?" she demanded, her gaze fixed to mine. "This magic is not yours to receive, as you well know. Only coven members are allowed to receive their heritage, and you, my dearest daughter, are a part of this coven no longer."

"I came to say goodbye to her," I argued. It was a truth—though my motivation had changed since meeting Peter.

Mother walked slowly toward me, her footsteps almost silent on the mossy ground. She tutted under her breath and wagged a finger in my face. "You don't belong here, Sarah," she chastised, her eyes flashing.

She stood in front of me, her eyes hard and furious. I looked at the other coven members. Maraud was watching me through dark lashes, her head bowed to her chest, but Geneva was the one I feared most. Her pitch black hair was heavy around her shoulders, the hint of blue a haze around her body and hanging like a cloak. They were chanting, all of them doing my mother's bidding. Saskia reached out for Devine's hand, who in turn reached for Geneva's, until the four of them stood in a circle as light danced about them.

I shuddered, feeling the tendrils of magic wrap around me.

The rain began to fall and the trees began to sway.

I began to shake, unable to stop.

Mother raised her hands to the sky, the blue magic she held glowing like fire in her palms.

I wanted to lift my arms to defend myself, but I feared any show of magic might send her over the edge. I was powerful and we both knew it. But there was no sense in inciting an all-out war.

"Please, Mother, you don't have to do this. I'm not staying. It's yours, all of it. I just wanted to pay my respects." My voice wavered. I hated how weak I sounded. Mother stood tall and terrible in front of me, the blue fire of her magic dancing dangerously in her hands.

"I believe you, daughter." She smiled patronizingly. "But I must insist on taking all of your magic so that you don't entertain the idea of coming back here ever again."

"I won't! I won't come back!" I pleaded, but it was pointless.

A bolt of lightning struck from nowhere and hit me between my shoulder blades.

I dropped to my knees and screamed again as burning agony ran through my body. It was everywhere, a fierce red-hot poker branding every part of me. I tried to lift my arms to defend myself, but found they were now locked by my sides.

"You will leave, and not come back." Her words reached me, even in the depths of my aching.

119

I blinked through the fiery pain and looked up at her. She stood in front of me, both hands over my body as they leached my magic from me, leaving me weak.

She was smiling. Happy to see me in so much pain. A small section of my heart broke away. Even though I knew she had always hated me, even though time and time again she'd proven her abhorrence, the small child inside of me still wanted her affection.

I glared up at her with my own hatred, once and for all murdering the child within me that still craved a mother's love.

Another bolt slammed through me, and more of my magic leaked onto the ground.

Geneva's words grew louder and Devine's humming hovered in the air like electricity, but I couldn't tear my eyes from my mother—the cause of so much of my suffering.

Mother's eyes fluttered, her mouth open and closing in what seemed to be ecstasy and agony all rolled into one. I blinked repeatedly but I couldn't see anything but blue fire all around me as she took some of her witch's strength and poured more and more electricity into my body. My power was entering her and I could hear her soft moans. I wanted to cry, but I couldn't make a sound.

I thought of Peter: forever locked in Grandmother's house, alone, my promise to him broken.

I wondered if anyone else would ever see him again after I was gone.

I thought about how much he would hate me for breaking that promise.

I thought of the loneliness that would eat away at him until he was only bitter and twisted and nothing of the man I could see beneath all the anger.

Inside I was screaming and begging for the forgiveness of Peter, this man that I did not know until two days ago, and yet now I felt like I had known him forever. Inside I was fighting and clawing, because I refused to give up.

Grandmother always said I had an inner strength that no one had ever seen before. She had tried for so long to access it, to help me use it somehow, but I never could—until now.

As I fell to the ground with my magic pouring out of me, I accessed this strength, thinking of Peter. Of how he made me feel. Of how I felt I had always known him—in this life, or another.

Closing my eyes against the blinding fire, I saw his face. I felt the heat from his touch and I refused to let her hurt me any longer. I pulled on every ounce of willpower I had inside me and I blocked my mother's power. I stopped her magic cold.

My own magic burned brightly, even brighter than hers. The power was so intense that she stumbled, almost falling over, and I was able to bring my hands up and surround myself with a protection spell meant to keep her at bay.

I got to my feet and glared down at her. She cowered before me, and we both knew that I could end her if I wanted to. I felt the black magic crawling up my spine, asking to be heard, but I refused to let it take hold of me.

"Stay away from me, Mother," I spat out and glared down at her.

The magic continued to pulsate from her, mixing with her violent anger, yet she stayed where she was, recoiling away from me. I glanced at the other witches, watching them as they stared back in surprise, forgotten magic burning in their fingertips. Saskia's face was frozen in shock, her mouth hanging open, her chant left dying on her lips.

I turned, still gasping in pain, and backtracked through the forest as quickly as I could, even as the hazy blue of Mother's electricity still buzzed through my body.

"You won't always be the strongest, Sarah!" my mother screamed after me, jealousy and anger tainting her words.

Ignoring her, I moved as quickly as I could through the woods until I collapsed at the edge of the trees. I lay there for only a few minutes, trying to calm my beating heart and ragged breath before dragging myself over to my jeep.

My hands fumbled for the keys, which I couldn't seem to get ahold of. So I flexed my fingers at the lock and used magic to open the door, and then I climbed in and used the same magic to start the engine before quickly backing out of the parking space and driving away from the cemetery.

# Chapter Thirteen

The wheels of my jeep screeched to a halt at the front of the house, but unlike when I had first arrived back in Raven's Cove, this time I did not hesitate in jumping straight out of the vehicle and running toward the front door.

It was not the ravens following me that I was frightened of, but faint memories resurfacing.

"Peter!" I called out his name as I threw myself inside the house.

Memories of Peter and I were flooding me. Images of him in my past. A past that I didn't recollect. They frightened me—he frightened me—and yet I welcomed them as the truth, as a fact of what had been.

\*

*"I don't care what they say, Sarah. I love you. How can that be wrong?" Peter's strong hands cupped my face, his eyes burning into mine.*

I reached up and pulled his hands gently away from my face. "I don't know..." I shook my head and looked away with an ache in my heart, "I don't want her to hurt you."

Peter laughed mockingly and I looked back up to him. He was strong and handsome, the faint shadow of a beard on his jaw.

Hardly anything like the boy I had grown up knowing.

"I'd like to see them try," he mocked, and I winced.

"Don't say things like that." I released his hands and turned away, barely taking a step forward before his hands wrapped around my waist and his mouth found my neck.

"You don't need to worry about me. You don't need to worry about anything." His feather-light kisses trailed up my neck until he slowly turned me back to face him. "I'll protect us both, Sarah. I'll do anything to be with you."

I believed him.

I believed every word that he uttered. But it wasn't as simple as that—as us defying our families' wishes.

We were not supposed to be together; our feelings were an anomaly.

He leaned down and pressed his lips to mine, and the beating of my heart sped up and the world fell away.

*He was right.*
*How could this be wrong?*


\*


My hair was a frenzy around my face, and my knees and hands were muddy and damp from the forest floor, but I didn't care, none of it mattered.

When I had been dying on the forest floor with my own mother draining my magic out of me, all I could think about was him. He had given me the strength to access magic that I had never been able to before. And he had given me the strength to fight back, to not give up.

Because after all these years, he himself had not given up.

"Peter!" I called to him again.

I ran through the lower part of the house, but didn't find him and so I climbed the stairs two at a time, calling his name frantically, like an echoing chant to the beat of my own heart. I called to him, and my voice hunted for his hiding place. "Where are you?"

But he didn't come.

No matter how many times I called for him or begged for him to come to me. I remained alone. I used an incantation to search for him, but since this was his prison, the spell merely revolved around the house, indicating that yes, he was there, somewhere, but he wasn't coming out.

I eventually sat on Grandmother's bed in defeat. Clasping her spell book in my hands, I flipped through the blank pages and begged for her magic to make its way to me so that I could finally see her spells.

I tried not to cry; it would do no good. I wanted to be strong and I wanted to understand what was happening—why I felt half crazed with the need to see him and feel him and know him. Why these images of him were haunting my subconscious.

Why I could feel his kisses, soft on my lips, and yet not remember them.

Why I could hear his words in my head and yet not know why he was saying them.

Why I knew that we had met before, yet I didn't know how.

I felt sick with memories inside of me that wanted to escape but were stubbornly refusing to come. Sick with knowing that my coven had destroyed his life, that they had prevented him from being free for so long. Sick with a longing for him that I didn't understand.

I hated them. I hated this. I hated how I was feeling.

I felt sick and angry and full of hate and anxiety.

Black magic rose inside of me like bile as my anger burned brighter and brighter.

"Peter…" I mumbled, pushing his name past my pursed lips.

"Sarah?"

I looked up sharply and he was there, standing in the doorway, his face devoid of emotion. I stood up as he moved toward me, and we slowly reached for one another across what seemed a wide expanse but was merely just existence, and not. Our hands did not touch, our fingers did not graze upon each other's skin, but I felt him all the same. He was my heart's other half. And like a thousand-year-old story being whispered into my ear, I saw and heard and felt his memories. Memories I did not have.

I tasted his pain and his anger and his love.

I saw my grandmother entrapping him to keep him from me. I saw her easy decision to choose me over him.

I looked up into Peter's face, clinging to the images in my head even as they tried to slip from my grasp.

Peter had been a good witch; he was my opposite.

He was white where I was black.

He was light where I was dark.

His coven was good and pure, and mine was not.

Separated, we were opposing forces, but together we were two pieces of the same puzzle, united. Together our magic had the potential to destroy everything. We shouldn't be, and yet we were.

I finally understood why my grandmother had kept us apart: it was fear, not love.

*

"Please, Violet! I love her!"

She shook her head sadly. "I told you to stay away. I told you but you wouldn't listen."

"How? How can you ask that of me? To stay away from her? She's everything. She's my reason for living, for breathing, for being. I can't live without her, Violet. Please, just give us a chance!" Peter reached for Violet but she moved out of his way.

"A chance? You want a chance?" she spluttered.

"Yes! Why is that so much to ask?"

Violet's shoulders sagged and she shook her head again. "You don't understand—neither of you understand."

"So help me to," Peter pleaded, his voice breaking on the final word. "I would do anything for her."

Violet looked up to him. "Anything?"

"Anything," he confirmed.

"You want to keep her safe, and yet it's you that will destroy her, Peter."

"No, never!"

"Yes! Don't you see? You're not supposed to be together." Violet opened her spell book and began flipping through the pages absently.

"We're opposites, I get that. But that doesn't mean our love is any less pure."

Violet looked up sharply. "Peter, know that you have done this to yourself. That you have damned yourself because you wouldn't listen to me. I have to do this to protect her."

Violet's magic glowed from her palms and Peter took a step back, his own magic glowing white in his own hands.

"I will protect her." He raised his chin in the air defiantly. Violet was coven leader, a strong and powerful priestess. His magic was nothing to her, and he knew it.

"The only way to protect her is to stay away. But you can't do that—won't do that, and so I must do what I see fit." She raised her hands up and released the magic from her fingertips. Some wrapped itself around Peter and some

130

*made its way out of the house and into the forest.*

*Peter cried out, falling to his knees. "Please, Violet," he begged, unsure what was happening.*

*Violet's plait hung down one shoulder and her crimson mouth opened as she uttered a chant. With each word spoken, Peter cried out as pain lashed at him. His wrists, his back, his ankles—he felt shackled. Imprisoned. He felt leaden down with magic.*

*At some point he must have passed out. The pain was too much. The suffering too painful.*

*He awoke with groggy eyes, realizing he was curled in a ball on the kitchen floor of Violet's house. His muscles ached as he tried to move, slowly shifting himself upright so he was sitting. He clutched at his head feeling groggy.*

*Violet was sitting at the table, sipping from a teacup and watching him.*

*"What did you do?" he asked, his throat feeling scratchy.*

*Violet put down her teacup. "You will remain here forever, Peter. Imprisoned in this house. No one but I will lay eyes upon you again. No one will hear your words or your cries. No one will remember you or your touch."*

*Her words stung like insect bites. "Sarah?"*

*"Sarah will no longer remember you."*

*The insect bites burned.*

131

*"I am sending her away from here, banishing her."*

*The insect bites gouged at his heart.*

*"You will never see her again."*

*The insects grew claws which plunged long-stemmed nails into his heart and ripped it from his chest.*

*"This is all there will ever be for you now, Peter."*

\*

Our hands hovered over one another's. We couldn't touch, but we were close enough as if we could. "I will get you out of here. I understand it now, Peter," I said.

I saw the memories, of my grandmother and of what she had done, and yet I still did not recall them as if they were my own. I saw how Peter felt, and I knew his feelings to be pure and true, but they were like watching someone else's story unfold. I did not know the Peter I saw in his mind. I did not know that man who would do anything for me.

"But you can't see her spells." He gestured toward the book, which was open on the bed, the starkness of the empty pages staring up at us both like a challenge, and he breathed out an exasperated breath.

"Grandmother's magic will come to me soon," I said.

"You aren't a part of the coven anymore. You can't get her magic, Sarah."

I pulled my cardigan to one side to reveal my raven brooch. It made me a part of the coven, meaning I would receive her magic like everyone else.

His eyes lifted to mine. "And then what?" he asked, the spark of hope in his eyes.

"Then we will leave here, together," I replied without pause, because for me there was no other way out of this.

"Together?" he said, the word a smile on his lips. "But…"

"Together, always," I replied, remembering his long ago promise to me. "I may not remember much, but I can feel what I know, and I know I belong with you."

He looked away, and I hated that. I wanted him to look at me, always. Though the feeling surprised me, I couldn't deny it any more than I could deny my lungs air. I might not have had my memories, but I was willing to trust in myself. I felt something for Peter—something that I didn't understand.

We held a connection, one my grandmother was willing to ruin people's lives for.

At some point Peter had loved me, and deep down I knew that at one time I had loved him back. I didn't have those feelings anymore, but I wanted to.

"Sarah, we'll destroy both of our covens. You know this?" He asked even though he could see the determination and resolve on my face.

Before that day I'm not sure if I would have taken a different path; would I have been willing to sacrifice everyone and everything I had ever known? My heritage, my ancestry, my coven and family—all of it would be wiped away with mine and Peter's union, and something new would be birthed.

After what I had seen in my mother's eyes earlier, I knew that yes, I was willing to sacrifice everyone for Peter—for what we might have been—just as they had sacrificed us.

Sacrifice is selfish, and it was something I had fought hard against, but there was no doubt in my mind that it was a sacrifice I was willing to make.

Perhaps it was the dark witch in me that wanted it, or perhaps it was all written beforehand. Regardless, I didn't want to be without Peter ever again—not now that I had found him. For many years I had felt like I had lost a part of myself, but the truth was that it had been stolen. Peter was that stolen part.

I didn't know if those memories would ever return, or if I could ever feel something like that for him again, but I was willing to try.

I nodded. "I know." The words tasted bad in my mouth, but I said them all the same, and I would say them again—a thousand times if I had to.

"I can't let you do this," he said, but his words were weak, as if he had been fighting them for as long as he could recall. And perhaps he had.

"You can't stop me," I replied, taking the decision away from him and erasing at least some of his guilt.

"I love you, Sarah." He lifted a hand and stroked a nonexistent touch down my cheek. "If I could kiss you right now, I would."

I imagined his touch, how it had felt earlier that day, and I tried to feel it again right then. Something had allowed us to touch previously, and I wished I knew what. Was it a break in the spell? Because Grandmother was dead now? Was the spell weakening? Or was it something else breaking through? A magic more powerful than my grandmother's, perhaps?

We both sat back down on the edge of the bed, both uncertain of when the magic would come to me. There was no specified timeframe. Sometimes it was minutes, other times hours. But I'd worn my brooch and I'd performed the ritual, so I would receive the magic, without a doubt.

The ravens were still outside; I could hear them squawking every once in a while, but they couldn't get in. They couldn't hurt me. I was safe, for now.

I lay back against the duvet, letting my legs dangle over the edge of the bed, and I looked at Peter. He turned around and smiled before lying down next to me, our bodies not touching and our hands not entwined, but I felt joined to him like I never had to someone before.

66 **W**e were in love?" I asked, finally breaking the silence between us.

He turned his head to look at me, a slow smile crossing his handsome face. "Yes, very much so."

"I wish I could remember more." I sighed.

"What do you remember?" he replied, lying down next to me.

136

I thought about that, about what I remembered of my own. But it wasn't much. A feeling of knowing him, of seeing him before, yet I didn't know where from. I had seen some of his memories, of the things he remembered, but for myself there was very little.

*Soft kisses, hot breath, and a thousand promises...*

"I remember my heart speeding up," I said, and turned to look at him. "I remember staring into eyes that were warm and made me feel safe and alive. I remember..." I touched my lips as ghosts' kisses warmed them, but the memory vanished before I could hold on to it. "That's it."

His eyes held such hope when I looked at him. "I have loved you since the day I first saw you." He reached over to stroke some of my hair away from my neck, but of course he couldn't, and his lips pursed in frustration.

He turned to face the ceiling once again, as if that was the end of our discussion. I leaned up on one elbow, my face hovering over his, and his smile grew wider.

"And when was that?"

He laughed, but it was a laugh I had not heard before. It wasn't a dark laugh, or a bitter laugh; this laugh was full of life.

"For most of your life I have been in love with you, Sarah." He stopped laughing and his

137

gaze caught mine. "I knew, even as children, that my heart belonged with yours."

My breath hitched in my throat as he held me with that gaze.

"I first saw you when your grandmother called a meeting with my father. Our covens were fighting, as they always were back then. You were barely twelve, and a gangly little thing." He smiled and then looked away, and his lower lip got trapped by his teeth as his face turned serious. "My father and your grandmother restricted us from even being friends. But even they couldn't keep us apart." He smiled at his own words, and I found myself smiling too. "There's something more that pulls us together. No matter what happens, we always find a way. It's something bigger than us. Bigger than everything."

I didn't know what to say in response, so we lapsed back into silence as my hazy memory caught around the image of two children running through the woods together, hand in hand, laughing. It disappeared like vapor as I watched it.

"Do you think I'll ever remember?" I finally asked.

His warm eyes, the eyes that I remembered so well yet didn't remember at all, watched me in silence, hurt dancing inside of them.

"I don't know," he replied. "But they haven't been able to keep us apart so far. So maybe it doesn't matter what you remember. Maybe it only matters that we're together."

I thought on his words a moment before replying. Deciding if it truly mattered to me that my memories had been stolen, a portion of my life just wiped away so easily and I decided that it did matter, and yet, I didn't care. What I cared about was what Peter had said.

It only mattered that we were together.

I barely knew Peter, and yet I knew that he was my future. He was who I was supposed to share my life with. All along I had been searching for something, for someone, and he had been right here—waiting for me to return to him.

# *C*hapter *F*ourteen

## Peter

I watched her fall asleep over an hour ago, and like I had done every night that she had been back at the house, I watched her in fascination and in awe. I had loved her deeply for ten years, yet I never thought we would get to this point. I never believed it possible that she would love me back. That we could ever be together.

Yet there we were.

Together, and yet not, but in love all the same.

She murmured under her breath and I leaned closer to hear what she was saying. But like the wind passing through the trees, the words were lost before they made it to my ear.

I was afraid for her and I was afraid for this next step that we had to take, together. I knew that in her heart she didn't want to harm anyone, that she was trying to be good, to let the darkness slip away from her, but I knew that she would do this, for me.

For so many years I had felt so much anger toward her family, and though I loved her, I'd felt that anger burning bright for her too. She hadn't been strong enough to remember me, and I had resented her because of that. Because she was all I had cared about, all I had thought about.

The anger and resentment had burrowed beneath my skin, through layers of muscle and bone, until it touched my soul. I knew how easy it was to get lost to that anger. At times I was still lost to it. I wanted them gone—her family. I wanted them obliterated. I wanted them to suffer, as I had, and that made me bad.

She didn't want to be bad, and I knew that she was fighting the black magic inside her, but I needed her not to—not to fight it. Her darkness was what made her *her*, though she didn't realize it. It was what made her powerful.

Her darkness was what I loved the most, just as my light was what she loved. We were the opposite in every way. We were each other's antonym, we were the anomalies of our family bloodlines, of our covens. But it was what we were made for, and the only way that we could be together. I understood that now. Violet had made it all clear.

Sarah was light within the dark and I was the dark within the light.

And we had to destroy each other to take the next step.

She murmured again, and I watched her lips moving. But it was almost painful to watch, because to watch them made me want to kiss them again. I squeezed my eyes closed, but all I could see was my mouth on hers. The urge to kiss her—to run my tongue along hers and let my hands explore her body as my tongue explored her mouth—was making me feel feverish. Her kisses were sweet and seductive without even trying to be, and she tasted like honeysuckle and lemon drops. It was the greatest goddamn taste.

"Peter?" Her voice broke through the insanity that was running through my mind, and I looked over at her. Her eyes were wide and beautiful and she was staring down at the side of her body. I followed her gaze and saw our fingers were touching—really touching.

I stared, uncertain, at our hands touching so innocently. The things that grew inside me would not be tamed or quieted, and as I looked up and my gaze met hers, I knew she was fighting the same war as I. Only, I could not fight this anymore. We were supposed to be together. For ever. We were made for one another.

*This was how the stars were aligned for us.*

When I couldn't ignore the calling of her heart to my own any longer, I pushed myself up to lean on one elbow, and, not wanting to waste another moment, I leaned down and gently kissed her.

And. I. Felt. Everything…

…*Everything!*

Every emotion I had ever felt for this beautiful woman. Every beat of my heart for her. Every kiss. Every touch. I felt it all.

It was like falling into heaven.

It was like coming home.

Her mouth was warm and delicious, and her tongue glided over mine, meeting my pace stroke for stroke. She reached her arms up to wrap around my body, and I moaned loudly against her mouth because the feel of her touch against me was more than I could wrap my mind around right then.

We were magnets, drawn to one another. And like magnets our bodies connected, fitting together like long lost pieces.

After nothing for ten years, a drought of feelings and touch, I was suddenly drowning in so much of it. I was drowning in her.

The room exploded in a flash of blue and a crackle of electricity. I had felt fear before, many times, but it was nothing like the fear I felt right now. I didn't want this kiss to ever stop.

Nor the silken feeling of her touch in my hair. Or her breathe against my face to disappear. I needed this—her—like I needed air. Like I needed skin and bone and breath in my lungs to exist. And if this ended now, before I was ready, then I was already dead. I would disappear into nothing, because my heart could not take the loss of her again.

The room burned brighter and brighter and she called out my name. One long groan of syllables on her lips as my name turned into something else. She began chanting, louder and louder, and then it wasn't me controlling our kisses, it was her.

# *Chapter Fifteen*

## Sarah

I couldn't see anything but Peter as the lyrical words trailed from my lips and my grandmother's magic poured into me.

I felt cold but on fire, I was there and yet I was somewhere else, I was with Peter in the moment, and yet I was seeing a thousand lives and a thousand tales unfold before my eyes.

My fingers burned and the magic ran through my veins like liquid ice, filling my every pore. I gasped as my lungs expanded with the power inside of me, and my arms flew out to either side of my body. My throat felt tight, so tight I could barely breathe, and then...

It was over.

My muscles relaxed, became soft instead of rigid. The crackling was replaced by the frantic beating of my heart and my own gasping breath.

I could feel my grandmother's magic inside of me. Her power, her devotion to the coven—

all of it. I could feel everything and everyone. I opened my eyes and saw Peter, seeing him and feeling him truly for the first time.

We were still kissing, our mouths still moving in sync with each other. His hands were on my face, clasping my face in his palms. He opened his eyes and slowly pulled out of the kiss, his gaze deepening and boring into my own.

"That was…" I didn't know what to say. How could I finish that sentence? That thought?

"Are you okay?" he finally asked, his voice thick and gravelly.

I nodded my ascent as I watched the bob of his Adam's apple.

"It was…" he began.

I nodded again. Because words couldn't describe what that was. It was amazing, frightening, bewildering, beautiful and yet ugly.

It was the truth and it was lies. It was freedom and imprisonment. It was everything.

It was Peter's turn to nod now, and it brought a smile to my lips. He watched my smile rise, and he matched it with one of his own. We watched one another, our bodies still entwined, our nerves still tingling with a thousand sensations. I could still feel him, his hands still holding me tightly, and his breath still hot on my face

"I should check her book," I said abruptly. Fear tingling down my spine and ruining this beautiful moment. "We won't have long before they come for me. If I got my magic then so did they, and now that they have the magic, they are powerful enough to get into the house."

He nodded and pulled away from me, though I could see his reluctance in doing so. I didn't blame him. I didn't want him to let go either.

I was nervous as I opened the book, scared in case I was wrong and inside it was nothing but blank pages and another broken promise to Peter. He reached over and placed a hand on my knee, a small shiver trailing down his spine as our bodies connected. But even as we were touching, I could feel him drifting away, his touch receding.

I flipped the cover open, seeing first only the blank, aged pages, but as my eyes adjusted and my gaze stayed fixed, the words became clear. I was scared to look anywhere but at the words forming in front of me, in case they vanished again.

"Peter."

"Can you see it? The spell, can you see the spell?" he asked, his voice sounding faraway and panicked. I nodded yes as more and more of the incantations appeared. Some familiar, others not so. I flipped through the pages quickly,

147

wide-eyed as each page filled, until I found the correct spell I was looking for.

"I can see it. I can see them all." My voice was shaky, and as he leaned over, wrapping his arms around my shoulders, I finally looked up, seeing bitter tears in his eyes.

Not just because I could see the words, but because, like his vanishing touch, I could barely see him anymore. He was disappearing right before my eyes, and his eyes held a fear like no other. Yes, I could see the spells, and yet I was now watching as he disappeared in front of my eyes, his mouth was moving but no words could reach me.

And finally I could see all of the spells, but I could no longer see him.

"Peter!" I screamed his name, staring around the room in shock. But he was gone, at least for now.

Whatever spell had allowed me to see him had been broken, and he was invisible to me like he was to everyone else. I clutched the spell book in my hands like his lifeline and I ran from the room, heading down the stairs and into the kitchen.

I read out the ingredients, searching through the shelves and cupboards until I found them all, and one by one added them to Grandmother's cauldron.

A squawk outside the window made me freeze for a split second, but I refused to turn and look; I knew what was there, who would be staring in at me if I did. Instead I ignored them and I focused on adding the herbs and plants into the potion one by one, grinding and crushing different ones into the pot until it was bubbling.

The ravens continued to come. By the sound of their squawks, their numbers had doubled and then tripled. But still I continued to ignore them—even as they pecked against the windows, their wings flapping against the glass. The room was darkening as they blocked out more of the light.

By the time the potion was ready, the sound of birds outside had built until it was almost a deafening roar. I set the spell book down next to the cauldron and began the incantation, letting my gaze finally travel outside and wishing immediately that I hadn't.

The view outside was wall-to-wall birds.

A mass of black and white, of doves and crows, of good and bad, all there to stop me before I ended their existence. It wasn't just my coven, it was Peter's also. No one wanted to die that day. And who could blame them? Not I. Not Peter. And yet, I could not carry on without him.

My heart shuddered in my chest and I wished with all my soul that I could see Peter right then, that I could feel his touch, his strength seeping into me, because right then I was frightened and I needed him.

If the spell failed, not only would he be lost forever, but so would I. I would be killed, at the hand of my own mother and her ravens.

And the tragic part was, Peter and I would never be together. Not even in eternity.

# Chapter Sixteen

## Peter

**M**y hand hovered over hers, not touching her at all, but there all the same. Like fog in the air, her fingers glided through me.

She couldn't feel me, but I was there, with her. Because no matter what happened, I wouldn't leave her. She was frightened. I could hear her heart thundering at a hundred miles an hour as if it were my own heart, and it pained me to think of her scared.

"You're okay, you can do this," I whispered to her. Though she would never hear my words I tried to reassure her all the same.

We would die being together, and I hated that with every ounce of my being. But I knew that she couldn't leave now, not without doing this—without freeing me. And I was selfish. I couldn't live without her anymore. I couldn't fight it anymore. I couldn't do any of this anymore.

And I knew that if she could remember me, she would agree to this too.

The birds outside the window were blocking almost all light from entering, and Sarah moved around the kitchen lighting candles one after another and placing them all around her.

She stood by the cauldron and took a steadying breath before beginning the spell. Despite her obvious fear, her long hair trailed over one shoulder, her dress was crumpled around the middle and her face was flushed. She had never looked so beautiful.

I watched over her shoulder, so close to her that she should have felt my breath upon her neck. She began the spell, the words coming effortlessly to her, like she had been using them her whole life, when in reality she had never uttered them before.

"Tesqouth simatri donara…" She threw some jasmine into the cauldron and the potion began to change color.

The first row of birds moved closer to the window until their bellies pressed against the pane and their beaks tapped over and over in an urgent attempt to break through the glass. The ones further back pressed against the front ones until they all looked angry and in pain.

They squawked and pecked and pushed forward. It wouldn't take much more for that glass to break and them to get inside.

The black of her family and the white of mine all mingled together until they were a mishmash of black-and-white stripes with beady eyes, combining to become something else altogether. Blood and feathers stained the window, fragile bones broke, and yet still they pushed onward.

Sarah's words were louder now, her voice almost a yell to be heard over the birds' screams as the house began to violently shake and shudder.

The candles toppled, setting alight the curtains at the kitchen window, the flames licking at the panes of glass and making the birds outside—our families—scream louder and louder, to get in but just as much to get away.

Only now it was life and death, and no one could leave until it was done.

Sarah was crying now, her hands trembling as she held them over the potion and dropped the last of the herbs inside. Her hair began to darken; beginning at the root and ending at the tip, it turned blacker than the night, and her eyes rolled back in her head. The little kitchen became a furnace of power and fire as the room began to swell. It expanded, almost snapping at the seams of existence until they were at breaking point, and then it contracted and shrank down to nothingness.

The room exploded into both light and dark until I couldn't see what was happening anymore. My hands, my feet, my face—they were all nothing, empty, devoid of anything but existing in that one singular moment.

Somewhere someone was screaming.

Somewhere someone was crying.

Somewhere everyone was dying.

As the life flooded back into me, my vision cleared and I saw a mass of feathers surrounding Sarah, droplets of blood flying from their beaks as they pecked at her body hard enough to draw blood.

I ran toward her, tearing at the birds and throwing them to one side, but it was no good: as I tore two away, three more would get in their place.

I called her name, my voice breaking free from within my own throat and escaping past my own lips.

I was real, I was there, I realized once more. She had set me free.

"Sarah!" I called for her again, and the body within the mass of birds stirred. She heard me! I raised my hands to the ceiling and called forth my own magic—magic that I hadn't been able to use in ten years but could now feel running through my veins and igniting my entire body once more.

"Hellath!" I roared, as bright white magic shot from my hands and poured down onto the birds.

They screamed, sounds of both human and bird melding into one, and then they fell away from her. The bodies lay mutilated and scorched on the ground next to her. Their deformed wings beat against the floor, trying to take them away, but they couldn't leave; I wouldn't let them.

Not after what they had done to my Sarah.

"Hellath, voyt traith!" I snarled as I got a glimpse of her beautiful face now forever damaged.

Fury burned through me as she blindly searched for me, her hands clawing out and her eye sockets bleeding, trailing red rivers down her cheeks. Her cries for me were so loud that it hurt my ears. I let go of my white magic and I embraced the darkness inside of me—a darkness that had been made forbidden, that I had fought against, and yet now I welcomed.

"Hellath, voyt traith!" The voice sounded unlike my own. It was deeper, rougher, and fiercer than I had ever sounded, yet like my dark magic, I encompassed it. I became it. "Hellath, voyt traith!"

The doves of my coven and the ravens of Sarah's at once burst into flames. I stepped forward and scooped her up off the bloodied floor, leaving the nest of bird bodies that had been beneath her to twitch and flounder, flames licking against their wings.

The fire began to devour the kitchen and everything in it as heat tore through the air, yet I stepped through the fire as if it were merely cool air.

Once outside I moved away from the house, heading away from the fire and deeper into the woods, where I lay her upon the forest floor and I knelt beside her.

Her salty tears mixed with the blood and I reached for her hand, taking it in mine and placing a kiss on her knuckles.

"You're here," she said through damaged, bloody lips, her voice sounding weak and yet happy. "You're really here."

I swept her hair back from her face, revealing more cuts and blood. "I'm here," I replied.

"Forever?" She coughed, and her whole face contorted in agony.

"Yes, I'm here forever now." I wanted to cry. I wanted to yell. I wanted to break things.

The anger grew inside of me, a tsunami of rage pouring through my veins as I stared down at my beloved Sarah.

But all I could do was hold her and offer her what little comfort I could.

"I saved you?"

I nodded, but then realized she could no longer see me. "You did. You saved me."

"I kept my promise." A smile touched her lips before falling away. "Peter, it hurts." Her chin trembled and I clung to her damaged body, pulling her onto my lap. I tenderly kissed her forehead and held her tighter.

"I know. I'm sorry, my love." I looked toward the house that was still burning. We only had moments left, and then it would all be over. Her pain, my pain, our covens, there would be something new after this. But I didn't know what. No one did. "Don't be afraid, I'm with you now." I squeezed her tighter.

"Always?" she asked.

I looked away from the house and back down to my beloved Sarah. "Always," I promised. "Always, my love."

I leaned over and laid a kiss on her lips, and I pulled her closer. Together. We were finally together.

## *C*hapter *S*eventeen

*U*nknown.

*I*n the ruins of a little house in the forest, there is a stirring—a shaking of earth and magic, of life and death, of good and bad. Within those ruins something grows, something bleeds, and something is born…

# $B$roken $M$agic

## Raven's Cove Series
## Book Two

*By USA Today bestselling Author*

*&*

*#1 Bestselling British Horror Writer*

*Claire C. Riley*

# Coming Soon!

**The Witching Hour Collection.**

Melanie Karsak – Witch Wood
Elizabeth Watasin – Charm School: The Wrecking Faerie
Eli Constant – Sleeping in the Forrest of Shadows
Blaire Edens – The Witch of Roan Mountain
Minerva Lee – Spun Gold
Evan Winters – The Witch of Bracken's Hollow
Erin Hayes – I'd Rather be a Witch
Carrie L. Wells – Playing With Magic
Claire C. Riley – Twisted Magic
Poppy Lawless – The Cupcake Witch

*Read on for the synopsis of another Witching Hour story by author Eli Constant:*

*'Sleeping in the Forest of Shadows'*

# *Sleeping* in the Forest of *Shadows*

## *SHADOW FOREST BOOK ONE*

By Eli Constant

**She has to abandon the world of light to truly live...**

When Tilda Brennen's family dies in a fire, she is left wheelchair-bound and suffering from survivor's guilt. It was her fault. She'd left the candles burning that night.

But there is a deeper, darker truth to the accident.

"He" has slept for years, dormant and untouched by the human world. Then she arrives at the little house beyond the woods and he awakens. He has waited so long for another chance. This time, he will not fail.

Going to the voice that summons her may heal

Tilda's body, but it will also cause her to lose everything she's come to love. And once she enters the forest of shadows, returning to human life might prove impossible.

Sleep here in the forest of shadows. Live inside the land of your dreams.

57017721R00104

Made in the USA
Charleston, SC
03 June 2016